BLACK WOLF RISING

A BERNADETTE CALLAHAN PREQUEL

LYLE NICHOLSON

BLACK WOLF RISING

BY LYLE NICHOLSON

Edited by Jessie Saunders of StormyNightPublishing.com
Book cover design by GetCovers
ISBN: 978-0-9959781-9-5

RED CULLIN PUBLISHING
Kelowna, BC"

1

SEPTEMBER 1993

BERNADETTE'S BOOTS thudded on the hard ground. Her chest heaving, lungs burning. Why had she chosen to run? She should have stood there, taken the beating in the schoolyard. It would have been over, teachers would have run out, broken it up—she would have suffered a bloody nose maybe, no problem.

But she'd kicked Tommy Cardinal in the groin. His grunt resounded around the reservation school. He'd called her father a white drunk—which was true. Then he called her mother an Indian whore.

Her foot had come up with its size-eight boot attached on its own, like a horse reacting to a slap in the hindquarters. The boot's reinforced toecap contacted Tommy's soft testicles, and he went down in a heap on the ground.

Bernadette had only seconds to stand over him grinning before Peter and Stephen Cardinal came rushing at her. They were Tommy's cousins, his guardians, and his muscle. Tommy was the mouthpiece, a scrawny seventeen-year-old, held back several times in grade school, to be the biggest pain in the ass at Lone Pine School for First Nations children.

If she'd have stood there, Peter would have smacked her, and

Stephen would have kicked her. Neither of them had the balls to beat her in the schoolyard. But she ran.

She headed down the path leading towards the river. The spruce trees swayed in the wind above her, watching her run, as if saying, "You're running into danger, turn back."

Peter and Stephen were gaining on her. They were taller, excellent runners, and both in running shoes, not boots. She dug in harder, sweat coming off her brow.

"You half-breed bitch," Peter yelled. "We're going to mess you up good this time, Bernadette."

A chill went down her spine. What would they do to her? The path to the river went downhill—she almost lost her balance, her heels dug into the hill as she descended in large leaps down the path. She could hear them breathing behind her.

She took a sharp right at the bottom of the path. There was a trapper's cabin there. Old Joe Two Feathers dried his fish there. He might be there. She'd be safe if he was.

The path narrowed. Wild rose bushes caught at her dress as she ran. Why the hell had she worn a dress? A dress with boots made her cool, but cool was stupid now. It slowed her down.

The cabin was in the distance. No smoke came from the chimney. A lump came in her throat. Joe wasn't there. She was on her own. Her boots dug into the dirt. If she could make it to the river, she could swim away from her pursuers. She was an excellent swimmer, while Peter and Stephen could barely swim.

The path to the river was past the trapper cabin. In thirty seconds she'd be there, in a minute she'd be in the river. She never made it. She tripped over a tree root, the big boots catching it squarely and sending her falling forward into the dirt.

The fall knocked the wind out of her. She tried to get up and found four hands on her. Her run was over.

Peter turned her over like she was a rag doll. His enormous face leered down at her. "Hey, Bernadette. Got you now, bitch."

She spat at him, bared her teeth in defiance. The last thing she wanted to do was show fear. Her fists balled in readiness to strike the moment they let her go.

Peter slapped her across the face. "You dare bite me? Thought you'd got away—you're going nowhere. Now, we'll teach you a lesson, you'll never forget."

"What...what're we... gonna do to her?" Stephen asked. It seemed a matter-of-fact question. He was out of breath trying to catch Bernadette and wondered what the spoils of the chase would be.

"We'll wait for Tommy," Peter said.

Tommy came limping down the trail. Bernadette glared at him. Her green eyes flashing at him as he came into view.

"You caught the piece of shit. Good," Tommy screamed as he came closer.

Bernadette fought Peter's grip, but he held her down with both arms, pinning her harder to the ground. "I'll slap you again, bitch," Peter said.

Bernadette eyed her surroundings, looking for weapons. There were rocks by the trail and a large broken branch. She took these in, judged their distance to her hands, and glared at Tommy.

"What're we gonna do to her, Tommy?" Stephen asked. "You want to get a long switch and give her ass a good few whacks?"

"Hell, no," Tommy said. "I think we're fixing to have an old-fashioned cock party." He smiled at Bernadette. "You know you've wanted me since you laid eyes on me. Now you got my attention. I'm all yours."

Bernadette spit a mouthful of blood from Peter's slap. "You think you're going to rape me, you got another think coming. I'll rip your dick off, you scrawny little shit."

"Damn it, Bernadette, this ain't rape, it's you giving the boys what they want in the woods. You know you've been longing for it. Who's going to believe a little half-breed bitch from a drunken white man and whorin' Indian woman?" Tommy asked in feigned surprise.

"Bastard," Bernadette screamed. She struggled against the grip of Peter and Stephen. They held her tight. "Pull up her dress and pull down her panties," Tommy yelled.

Peter changed his grip on Bernadette. He pulled on her dress. Her arm came off the ground. "Quit squirming, Bernadette," he yelled.

Tommy pulled his zipper down and realized he had a problem. Bernadette's kick to his testicles had produced a negative lift off in his erection. He put his hands down his pants, but nothing was being aroused.

"God dammit. She kicked the life out of my dick," Tommy said. "Peter, I'll hold her, and you do her, then Stephen can have at her, and my dick will be back in action."

"Sure thing," Peter said.

Tommy came to Bernadette's side. Her legs were thrashing with those deadly boots. Her long, light-brown legs were showing up to her panties. The boys were licking their lips for the prize they were about to partake.

When Peter let Bernadette's arm go for Tommy to take over, Tommy wasn't fast enough to grab hold. Bernadette shot from his grip. She punched Stephen in the nose with her fist. He yelped and fell over.

She rolled off the path and picked up a rock and came at Peter's head with it. Peter was beside Tommy, his back to the bushes. He lifted one arm—too late. The rock hit Peter's head in a sickening crunch.

Bernadette grabbed the tree branch on the path, holding it high over her head, aiming it at Tommy. Tommy put his hands up in defense. She stomped on his leg with her boot. He screamed in agony and grabbed his leg. The branch came down hard on his head.

Stephen lay there, wild-eyed on the trail. "Don't hurt me, Bernadette...please...I was just along...you know...to have a little fun."

"You pathetic asshole," Bernadette screamed. She hit him hard with the branch on his body; he turned away, and she landed one on his skull. The crack of branch on bone told her she'd found her mark. He collapsed on the ground.

Bernadette stood over the three bodies. Were they just knocked out? Had she killed them? She couldn't care less. They wanted to rape her. If she had a knife right now, she'd have cut their dicks off and hung them around her belt like scalps, tribute to her victory.

She let out a bloodcurdling Indian war whoop, running down the trail and back towards her home. There would be consequences for this fight, there always were in the tiny village. She had no idea this would change her life forever.

2

MORNING ARRIVED with a thunderstorm booming in the distance and a loud knock on the door. Bernadette's grandma Moses went to answer the door. She did it in the same manner she did everything, which meant in her own time.

Nothing pushed Grandma Moses except the seasons. She opened the door to stop whoever at the door was pounding on it.

Chief Dan Cardinal stood on the small wooden step. He looked larger than normal. This morning he was wearing his cowboy hat instead of his baseball hat. The cowboy hat meant he was on official business.

Grandma Moses waved him into the house and went to her wood stove to make tea. She always served tea the moment you walked into the house. You could ask for something else, but it would appear as tea.

Chief Dan followed Grandma Moses into the house and sat at the kitchen table. It was the only place to sit. Off the kitchen was a postage-stamp-size living area with an armchair, coffee table, and small television with antennas that searched in vain for fuzzy reception from down south. Grandma Moses was the one who sat in the armchair.

"There's been a problem," Chief Dan said, after clearing his throat a few times. He felt uneasy around Grandma Moses. The whole native village knew she could channel spirits. No one messed with her unless they wanted an ill omen to descend on them.

"What kinda problem?" Grandma Moses asked.

"Tommy, my boy, and his cousins, Stephen and Peter, they got beat up bad down by the river," the Chief said. His big body creaked forward in the little kitchen chair.

Grandma Moses poured the tea into cups and placed a cup for the chief. "Oh," is all she said.

"The boys say Bernadette was at the river," the chief said.

"Is that so?" Grandma Moses said as she shuffled over to the table and sat down. She didn't look a match for the chief, but she was. Grandma Moses was small, plump in the middle, and always dressed in the same shapeless, flowered dress. Her grey hair had been grey since Bernadette could remember. It had two styles, tightly woven pigtails, either up or down.

But it was her eyes. The soft brown eyes registered her slight surprise or interest with the smallest flicker. They could pierce into the heart of the biggest men and make them uneasy.

Bernadette stood in the bedroom's doorway she shared with her grandma. She could see the chief squirming.

The chief looked away from Grandma Moses and stared at Bernadette. Their mutual hatred for each other was apparent. Bernadette held his gaze and stared back at him.

"Tommy says you led Stephen and Peter to the river and some white boys from town jumped them. You want to tell your Grandma and me why you did it?" the chief said.

Bernadette held her hand to her mouth. She couldn't believe what she was hearing. Of course, how could those three idiots explain how they'd been beat up by a sixteen-year-old girl?

The chief stared at Bernadette, then looked back at Grandma Moses. "it involves the RCMP. They'll be out to question Bernadette. Look here, Grandma Moses, no one wants trouble here, but your Bernadette has brought it on herself—"

"Ha, bullshit," Bernadette yelled.

The chief winced. No one interrupted him. He could expel anyone who did it on the reservation or in council. Under the gaze of Grandma Moses, he was on shaky ground..

"I'll speak with her," Grandma Moses said. She got up from the table. The meeting was over. The chief knew it was time to leave. He put his hat on with determination, adjusted its brim, and then lumbered out the door. He slammed it as his last act of authority.

"Why didn't you tell me this last night?" Grandma Moses asked. It wasn't accusatory, just a question.

"I thought you'd think I was stupid for running from them. I shouldn't have run. Tommy called Mom a whore, so I kicked him in the balls then ran. They chased me into the woods, caught me, and said they were going to rape me..." Bernadette's voice broke as she explained.

Grandma Moses walked over and held Bernadette. She was much smaller than Bernadette, but her embrace was strong. "I'm glad you got the better of them." She stared up into Bernadette's eyes. "You should have cut their balls off."

"I didn't have a knife," Bernadette said.

A knock came at the door. Bernadette went to the door and opened it to find RCMP Sergeant McNeil at the door. She motioned for him to come in. Dryness came into the back of her throat. The lie the boys had told was manifesting ominously.

"Thanks for seeing me," the sergeant said.

As Bernadette closed the door, she could see the locals crowding around outside. She was already guilty. The crime was bringing in white boys to do her dirty work.

Sergeant McNeil looked like he'd dropped into the world, old and worn. His hair and mustache were grey, his eyes were a washed-out blue, and the man had a roadmap of worry on his wrinkled face. It was like the world's problems had settled on him and wouldn't let go.

McNeil sat at the table and removed his hat. He took out a notepad and pen and laid them out on the table. "I'm here to take your granddaughter's statement. There are no charges being laid; we need to find the facts."

Grandma Moses sat across from McNeil, shoved tea towards him. "You want to tell me what facts you're dealing with?"

McNeil raised an eyebrow at her question. He should have known Grandma Moses would cross-examine him. He'd been here several times before when Bernadette had gotten into trouble in town. He leafed through his notebook and read. "The Cardinal boys stated they chased Bernadette into the woods after she assaulted them. Deep in the woods, several boys from town jumped them and beat them unconscious."

"Bullshit," Bernadette said.

Grandma Moses put up her hand to silence Bernadette. "Tell me, Sergeant, do you believe this report?"

McNeil shook his head. "Not a word. All the teenage kids from town were away at a basketball game in La Crete. I checked with sick reports, and I have two scrawny twelve-year-olds in town. I don't think they were a threat."

"You know the Cardinal boys are lying. Why come here and make like you're on their side?" Bernadette said. She fixed her gaze on the constable with her arms crossed.

"Because I needed to talk to your grandma and you, Bernadette," McNeil said. He stirred his tea and looked across at Grandma Moses. "You know the village will discover the boys lie—don't you?"

Grandma Moses nodded her head.

McNeil continued, "they'll come after Bernadette harder next time. I'm sure whatever happened in the woods wasn't good—"

Bernadette unfolded her arms and stepped forward, "They tried to—"

"Stop!" Grandma Moses commanded.

"Did they assault you... sexually?" McNeil asked. His eyes dropped to the table with his question. He hated dealing with rape cases. They had no female officer in their detachment; it always fell on him to do investigations into rape. He was terrible at it. He was so uncomfortable in the interviews with women that few wanted to offer allegations.

Grandma Moses threw a threatening glance at Bernadette. She got the message. Her lips tightened so hard they went white. She held back a tear, trying to escape from her eye.

"Bernadette has no statement to make other than she saw nothing," Grandma Moses said.

"I leave this up to you." McNeil sighed and put away his notebook. He looked up at Bernadette. "No one ever takes the RCMP's advice, but if I can say one thing, it's get this girl out of here."

"But I didn't bring any white kids in to beat them up," Bernadette protested.

"Doesn't matter," McNeil said. "The town is already up in arms because they know it isn't true, and your reservation is ready to have me arrest Bernadette because they think it is true."

"Where's my justice?" Bernadette said.

"You shamed Chief Cardinal's son and his cousins," McNeil said. "It's your word against theirs, and they've got bruises to prove their case. Bernadette, you'll never be safe here."

"He's right, Bernadette," Grandma Moses said. "The Cardinal boys have many friends tougher than they are. If they can convince them you ambushed them, you're in big trouble." She turned to look at McNeil. "I'll send her away tomorrow."

Sergeant McNeil got up and headed towards the door. "I'm sorry it had to be this way, but perhaps it's for the best." He turned and looked at Bernadette. "Sometimes a fish becomes too big for its pond."

Bernadette stood and faced her Grandma. "What's he saying?"

"He's right. I'm going to make a phone call. Pack a bag."

3

THE RAIN WAS FALLING. Dark clouds overhead were promising an endless supply of fall moisture that would soon turn to snow. Bernadette stood close to her grandma as they waited for the Greyhound bus.

An elderly couple eyed them over the brims of their coffee cups. Bernadette stared them down, then looked away. She was used to the looks. She had reddish hair, was tall with light brown skin and green eyes. Her Cree Heritage was always fighting with her Irish mix. In the summer it was worse. The sun made her hair turn a telltale bright red, and freckles appeared on her face and arms of their own accord.

On the reservation, she stood out. A baked potato they called her, brown on the outside and white on the inside—the least hurtful insult they threw at her.

Bernadette stamped her feet to relieve the tension she felt at being sent away. She was going to Aunt Mary's in Edmonton, the largest city in the north, over 600 kilometres to the south. There had been a nasty argument between her mother and Aunt Mary many years ago. She had no idea what it was, but when Grandma Moses told Mary she was taking Bernadette in, there was no argument.

The bus arrived. She hugged her grandma fiercely and grabbed her pack to get ready to get on the bus.

Her grandma held onto her arm. "I had a dream about you last night."

"What kind of dream?" Bernadette asked.

"I saw you standing tall. There was a big leaf behind you—it was red, and you were wearing red," Grandma Moses said.

"What do you think it meant?" Bernadette said.

"I'm not sure," Grandma Moses said, "but I want you to promise me you'll finish high school. It's what your mother asked me to do for you before she died."

"I promise," Bernadette said. She didn't want to say it. She was hoping to bolt from Aunt Mary's soon after she arrived there. Now, she'd made a promise she couldn't break, not to her grandma, not to her dead mother.

Bernadette climbed on the bus, choosing a seat by the window, dropping her backpack on the aisle seat beside her. She wanted no company on the ten-hour trip south. Anyone attempting to take the seat would get a fierce glare.

The bus's engine whined, the pneumatic brakes blew, and it pulled onto the highway gaining speed. Bernadette watched the trees go by faster and faster until they were a blur. She slouched down in her seat, pulling her Sony Walkman from her pack and putting on her headphones. She was debating whether to start with something from Stone Temple Pilots or Alanis Morissette and her recent song, "Ironic."

She chose "Ironic." Looking out the window, she saw Tommy, Stephen, and Peter. They stood beside the road. Bandages covered their heads like white turbans.

She wanted to laugh at them. They raised a fist and pointed at the bus. She knew it wasn't over between them. It would never be over.

4

THE BUS TOOK its own sweet time on its journey south. There were stops to pick up and drop off passengers in High Level, Paddle Prairie, Manning, and Peace River before they stopped for lunch. Then, as if the bus protested, they lumbered off farther south to Valleyview, Fox Creek, and White Court.

Somewhere around Mayerthorpe, another small town with nasty restrooms and tepid tea, she thought about her past. Her life had been Gypsy-like. Her five brothers were a vague memory. They hardly kept in touch. They'd been born and scattered like seeds in the wind to other relatives.

Bernadette had traveled from town to town with her mom and dad, living in motels, a camper van and sometimes a parked car, pursuing their country western music stardom. A wonderful dream that had caught Bernadette in its spell until one day it crashed to the ground. The music stopped.

Her sixteen years of travel had given her a tough shell and an unwillingness to let people into her confidence. Her life on the road ended with the memories of her mother and father on stage in some tavern in yet another small town. The music had died, and so had something inside of her.

She'd become used to getting by and standing up for what she wanted. This Edmonton trip was just another detour in her life's journey. One day soon, she'd be on her own and making her own decisions. The day couldn't come fast enough.

The bus pulled into an industrial area of west Edmonton. The driver announced the stop. Passengers rose slowly, pulling luggage from the overheads and shuffling from the bus. Bernadette lingered, then followed.

Aunt Mary's scowl on meeting Bernadette was colder than the evening air. Bernadette was being forced on her by Grandma Moses —her body language said it all.

Aunt Mary wasn't as good looking as Bernadette's mother had been, but she had a pleasant, round face with soft brown eyes and full lips. She was as tall as Bernadette with long, flowing, black hair falling to her shoulders. Her grandma once said she could have been somebody, but some trouble got in the way. She never explained what it was, just left it to hang there like a question mark. Perhaps it was something unspeakable.

They got into a taxi. The trees still had leaves, not like the ones in the Bernadette's far north village, which had shriveled to brown and flown away, and there was still light in the evening sky. They drove from the industrial part of town into a more residential side with row upon row of low-rise apartment buildings.

Bernadette watched out the window with interest at the neat two- and three-story apartments they passed and wondered what place her aunt lived in. She hoped it might be an upscale one. The one they pulled up to was anything but.

Her aunt's apartment was old and run down. The carpets in the hallway were threadbare and filthy. The light fixtures overhead shone a faint glow through the dirt, and dead bugs piled inside the lenses.

Bernadette was glad the lights were so dim; she could only imagine how bad the walls looked in the light of day. They entered Aunt Mary's apartment and her two little cousins, Abigail and Amber, greeted her in the doorway.

She dropped to her knees and hugged them both. "My god, I haven't seen you in years."

"Do you remember us?" Abigail asked. She was the prettier one, almost seven, with intense brown eyes and dark hair sweeping over her round face.

"Of course I do," Bernadette said. "You came to visit Grandma Moses and me three years ago."

"We did?" Amber asked. "I don't remember." She peered at Bernadette sideways, as if not sure what to make of this tall teenager at the door.

"You were six," Bernadette said. She looked up at her Aunt Mary. It was a tough visit, the year her mother passed away. Her aunt looked away.

"You hungry?" Aunt Mary asked.

Bernadette had thought little about food but realized she'd eaten little on the bus trip. The food her grandma had given her was moose meat jerky and bannock bread. Moose jerky was tasty, but it stunk to high heaven in close quarters. She hadn't felt like pissing off the other passengers. She nodded at her aunt.

Her aunt made her some mac and cheese and poured her a glass of milk, then put the kids to bed. She sat across from Bernadette, pouring herself a coke.

"We got to get some things straight, kid,"

Bernadette swallowed hard, "Okay...what do we need to talk about?"

"I agreed to take you in because you can help with the kids at night." She took a big swig of her coke and looked at Bernadette to see if she was following, "You see...I've been serving breakfast at the tavern down the road. It's not much of a tavern, a real shit hole, but I can make good money and tips on the evening shift serving drinks."

"You want me to look after Abigail and Amber after school?" Bernadette asked.

"You got it. You're a smart kid, here's a list of swimming pools and soccer fields they go to after school. I expect you to take them."

Bernadette shrugged. She didn't mind being with the children in the evenings. Her grade twelve studies were on her mind. She'd promised her dying mother and her grandma she'd finish high school.

"Good, Look, we may have gotten off to a poor start...well, maybe I did. I didn't give you much of a welcome when you arrived. As you can see, my place isn't much to look at..." She waved her hand around the small apartment to make her point.

Bernadette shrugged again. It seemed like an okay response to make.

"And as for sleeping arrangements, you get the couch. I'll need the bedroom with the girls to sleep when I get home at one in the morning."

"Sure," Bernadette said. She assumed when she saw the place, there was just one bedroom, someone would get the couch; she figured it would be her.

"Great," Aunt Mary let a small smile grace her lips. She'd expected a blow up with Bernadette. "Here's your school's address. It's seven blocks away. You'll drop the girls off at their elementary school on your way. I start my evening shifts at the tavern tomorrow."

"I got it, Aunt Mary, I'll leave for school early and take the kids to school," Bernadette said. She had decided she would do whatever her Aunt Mary asked. She'd put herself into this situation—she had to deal with it.

"Good. And one more thing, your school has a reputation for being tough. Promise me you won't get into any trouble. You hear me?"

Bernadette shrugged, then nodded. Trouble always had a way of finding her. She'd deal with it when it arrived.

She didn't sleep well during the night. The couch was okay; the pillow was nice, but it was the noise. She could hear the people in the next apartment. The walls seemed paper thin, toilets flushed, televisions droned, and cars swished by on the street in the rain.

Going to a new school didn't bother her. In her travels with her mom and dad, she'd either been home schooled or attended some school for a year or two, then they'd move on.

Her mother's death had deposited her at the Lone Pine Native reservation school. She'd been to schools on Vancouver Island, the interior of British Columbia, and a few towns in Alberta.

Her mom and dad were wannabe musicians.They were the Travelling Callahans, and Bernadette had loved every minute of their life on the road together. She'd listen to her mother's voice that some compared to Shania Twain blend in harmony with her father's lilting Irish brogue and get transported to a different world. One that didn't smell of stale beer and cigarettes.

Her father's descent into alcohol had torn the band apart. Bernadette had been there to see her mother's descent into depression and death from a broken heart.

Bernadette sighed as all these thoughts came to her. A loud siren from a police car or ambulance broke her train of thought. She fell into a troubled sleep and hoped she could stay away from trouble to complete her schooling and her grandma's and mother's wishes.

5

BERNADETTE WOKE from a deep sleep to see two pairs of brown eyes peering at her. Abigail and Amber stood over her, smiling. "Mom said you'd make us breakfast," they said in unison.

She rubbed the sleep from her eyes, made her way to the bathroom and then to the kitchen. After much discussion, they settled on Eggo waffles and fruit.

Bernadette found herself some bread for toast and made tea. She surveyed the small apartment, shaking her head at how grim it looked. There were few pictures on the wall, the furniture was old and looked like they had recovered it from garbage bins. She wondered just how bad off her aunt was.

She made sandwiches for the girls for lunch and one for herself, then threw her stuff into a small backpack and got ready for school. She dressed in black jeans, a black t-shirt, and pulled on her big boots with the heavy toecaps, and threw on a denim jacket.

"You look tough," Abigail said.

Bernadette smiled. "Yeah, you never want to look like the weakest wolf in the pack on your first day."

"What does it mean?" Amber asked.

"It's just something your Grandma Moses says," Bernadette said.

They marched to the girl's school.

Bernadette dropped the girls off, introducing herself to the teachers so they knew she'd be picking them up after. A concerned look from the teacher had Bernadette giving them her aunt's name and work phone number in case they wanted to check on her.

Fifteen blocks later Western High appeared. Her aunt had been way off about the distance. It was big, much bigger than Bernadette had ever attended. A foot-ball and track field bracketed the three-story brick structure surrounded by high fences. Bernadette had seen some better-looking prisons.

Cars and trucks stopped in front, jettisoning high school kids in various states of dress and attitude. Bernadette walked up the front steps, found her way to the administration office, and announced herself.

An officious-looking lady with large glasses and a home dye job turned a strange green shade listened to Bernadette's story before saying, "You're transferring from where?"

"Lone Pine First Nations High," Bernadette said in a confident tone. She didn't expect anyone had ever heard of it or the little town of Fort Vermilion some twenty minutes' drive from it.

The officious looking lady's name was Ms. Shibanov, and she scowled at Bernadette. "Just a minute, let me get the school counselor."

She ushered her into a small office with a trim-looking lady, approaching late thirties in a polyester pantsuit and a blonde pony-tail stretched back so tight it looked painful. Trendy, wire-rim glasses with square lenses and a mild tint shaded her eyes. No ring adorned her finger; she tapped a pencil in her left hand. Bernadette had her pegged as a hopelessly unmarried type with three cats at home.

Her desk plate read Ms. Blacksburg. "Do you have transcripts from your last school?" she asked.

"Ah...no..." Bernadette answered, "my transfer was kind of sudden..."

"You in some kind of trouble?" Blacksburg asked.

"No, you can check with Sergeant McNeil of the Fort Vermilion

RCMP, I have no record, and they have never charged me with anything," Bernadette said. She recited it almost as if she was a lawyer for a defendant.

Ms. Blacksburg jotted down the names of the school and Sergeant McNeil. "Please wait outside, Bernadette, I want to make some calls."

Bernadette sat in the outer room. She sat as close to the door as she could to hear the telephone conversation. A faint murmur of conversation came through the door, but she couldn't make anything out.

Many scenarios rocketed through her brain. Had the Cardinal boys convinced the RCMP to file charges? Did they find some kids from town to go along with their stupid story? Should she run? Head for the bus station? Where would she run too, who would hide her?

The counselor opened the door. She had a smile on her face. "Come on in, Bernadette, everything's fine."

Bernadette came in and sat down across from the counselor. Relief washed over her. It almost made her feel dizzy.

"RCMP officer McNeil explained the situation," Blacksburg said, and then paused. "You seem to have a penchant for trouble, young lady—you think you'll continue it here?" Her eyebrows knitted into an accusing frown with the words.

"Ah, no, I don't think so. There were some problems...some people there..."

"—Didn't like you because you weren't a true first nation's status, Cree?"

"Yes, I'm Métis, my mother was Cree and my father Irish. Some people on the reservation didn't like my mix," Bernadette said.

"And both your parents have passed away?" Ms. Blacksburg said. The way she said it, Bernadette knew she'd gotten the complete low down from her old school.

"Yes, my grandma took care of me on the reservation after my parents'...ah...death, and I'm living with my aunt Mary now, her last name is Landry," Bernadette said.

Ms. Blacksburg made notes, having already produced a file folder for Bernadette with a student number. She looked up at Bernadette, her eyes going into her already-familiar frown. "You realize the difficulty of transferring from a first nations school to a Canadian public school, don't you?"

Bernadette smiled weakly. "I've been transferring to and from first nations to public schools since grade four. I realize there's a big difference, and I've been able to keep up. I was in public school last year, here are my marks from that school."

She took her marks from her backpack and handed them to Ms. Blacksburg, who perused before finally saying, "You did very well there, it's too bad you moved around so much."

She didn't want to explain how many times she'd moved from town to town with her parents. Sometimes they'd settle in a town, and then her father would drop her off at grandma's house for a while as he *"sorted things out,"* which meant he went on a massive drunk.

"Here are the courses you'll be taking," Ms. Blacksburg said. "You shouldn't have a problem with these; however, math will be tougher this year. Decide on your electives, and we'll get you started tomorrow."

Bernadette studied the list. There was Math, English, Social Studies, Chemistry, and French. She'd have to fill in some Physical Education and an arts course to round it out, but it was doable.

"Did your aunt or grandma give you money for books?" Ms. Blacksburg asked.

"Not as yet...I'll get it," Bernadette said. She didn't want to meet her gaze. Her grandma had the money for her bus fare. Aunt Mary was barely keeping the squalid apartment over their heads.

"Well, here's a list of the books. The bookstore down the hall has some used editions on at a reasonable price. If you need help, you come back and see me. We have a student aid program."

"Thanks, I won't be needing it." She'd already seen her source of income on the way into school.

"Fine, here is your temporary student card. You must get your picture taken for your permanent one, your home room is with Ms.

Prefontaine in 3011, and you'll start tomorrow morning. Questions?" Ms. Blacksburg asked.

"None," Bernadette said. She smiled and walked out of the office, winking at Ms. Shibanov. She had her class schedule and book list. It took her a moment to orient herself to a school of this size, but she made her way towards the parking lot and found the thing she was looking for. A poker game. To her, it was better than a bank machine —it gave out unlimited cash.

6

BERNADETTE SCOPED the school before she'd entered the administration office. She saw the groups to watch out for: those dressed in the torn jeans and plaid shirts with leather jackets were the grunge group. They were all fashion and nothing to worry about.

A small group of kids dressed in black jeans, black t-shirts, and denim jackets with big boots looked tough. And kind of scary. When she'd walked by she'd seen all eyes on her, checking her out; was she a threat, or could they could recruit her?

Her goal was to keep her distance from them for as long as possible until she could find some allies. Someone to guard her back when this group came looking for her, and she knew they would.

Bernadette avoided the scary group and made her way out a back door to where she'd seen some girls playing cards. She'd been playing poker since she was six years old. Her dad, Dominic Callahan, had taught her the game. It amazed him how quickly she caught on.

She was a natural card counter and could read the tell on another's face like a map. "She's a natural!" Her father would call out to her mother as Bernadette once again bluffed with a pair of twos.

"Don't make it look too easy," her father would say. "You need the marks to think you're sweating a bit, raise the stakes slowly, then go for the kill."

Bernadette approached the girls on the ground. "Whatcha playing?"

A big girl looked up, brushing the hair out of her eyes. "What's it look like, dumb ass. We're playing poker."

"Oh," Bernadette said, "I've played poker a few times."

"Wanna join us?" a small girl in jeans and sweatshirt said. She elbowed the big girl and said something to her. The big girl giggled.

"You want to play?" the big girl asked. She did it nonchalantly, as if it meant nothing to her, but there was a look around the group they'd found a mark.

"Sure," Bernadette said, adding a shrug as if she'd be happy to get fleeced by these three.

She sat on the ground; they dealt her in, told her what the game was and what cards were wild, and it was a five-dollar minimum to ante in.

Bernadette suppressed a smile. Most groups tried to reel her in slowly, like a dollar in, and a two-dollar raise. These girls were greedy.

She let them think they had her for the first few hands. Huffing out her breath and holding her hand to her forehead in feigned concentration, she watched them as they become bolder with their bets.

When the pot had hit one hundred dollars, she drew a full house. "I think my cards are better than yours, am I right?" she asked in mock surprise.

"Goddam rookie," the big girl said.

Bernadette made a weak smile and threw in a shrug to mask her surprise. Her next hand had nothing. She took two draws with no luck. This was now her main game, bluffing.

The other girls were watching her intently. Bernadette let her eyes grow wider at each draw, saying nothing but trying to mask her delight at cards she supposedly had.

The other girls ran the pot to fifty dollars, then folded. Bernadette didn't let them see the cards they had dealt her, she didn't have to. But for now, she'd made enough money from this group of marks.

"I need to go, girls, I've got to get my books before the store closes. Thanks for the card lesson. Hopefully, I'll come back and you can teach me some more."

There were mutterings from the girls as she left the parking lot. Bernadette tried not to laugh out loud. They'd be good for at least a month before they caught on.

She ran back into the school, found the bookstore, and shelled out sixty bucks for the five used textbooks, a notebook, pencils, and a lock for her locker. A glance at the clock showed she still had an hour to kill before she picked up her cousins.

The school needed some checking out. She stashed her books in her locker to look around. She'd never been in such a large place before. After walking down the long hallways, she found her home room would be and the gym, which reminded her she'd need running shoes and shorts.

Bernadette decided she'd seen enough of the school. She pushed through the big outside doors and ran straight into the scary group.

"Hey, you!"

The hair on Bernadette's head stood on end. Her fists clenched. She continued walking.

"Hey, you, with the red hair and boots, I'm talking to you."

There was no way she was going to get away from this group. There were five of them, three girls and two guys. Cigarette smoke billowed from their midst, their eyes glaring through the mass of hair hanging down over their foreheads.

Bernadette stopped and turned. "You like my boots? I got these last year at the Army and Navy store, pretty rad, huh?"

A stocky, dark-haired girl made her way from the group. "Don't be smart with me, bitch."

Bernadette smiled. "Sorry, but I don't know you, so kind of wondered what the fuss is about." Her first defense would be tact. Her father always said to reason with an "*ijidt*", which was Irish for idiot.

"Fuss, you want to know the fuss?" the dark-haired girl said. "You're wearing our colours. You got that? No one comes to this school wearing our rags without paying respect."

"Oh, sorry. Look, I'm new here, just arrived, so I didn't know the code," Bernadette said.

"You better know it, bitch, and learn it fast, otherwise I'm like to be laying a *whopping* upside your head," the dark-haired girl said. The girl wore tight black jeans, black t-shirt barely covering her midriff, and a jean jacket. Black boots with chains that jingled when she walked. Her face was broad with a ring in her nose and one above her eye. Bad makeup highlighted the blemishes on her face.

Bernadette suppressed a grin. This girl was trying to sound like a gang member from East Los Angeles; had no one told her she lived in Northern Canada?

"Okay, got it, thank you," Bernadette said. She turned and continued walking down the steps and onto the sidewalk.

"Hey, *waitaminute*. I ain't don talkin' whiff you yet." The dark-haired girl said.

Bernadette stopped and cringed. The girl was now acting out some gangsta fantasy in front of her friends. She could either play along with it or make a stand.

The girl came jogging up to her, out of breath. It annoyed her she had to catch up to Bernadette to berate her more. She looked left and right at her pack to see if she was doing the right thing. They were watching with interest—nothing like a girl fight to round out a boring afternoon of cutting classes.

Bernadette turned and faced the girl. "Look, I have places to go, I have to pick up my cousins from school. How about we do this another time?"

The dark-haired girl's head shot back. "What you saying? Do what another time? You want to mess with me later. No way, bitch, we do this now."

How Bernadette had stepped into a fight with this girl, she wasn't sure. But unless she wanted to get slapped around, she needed to stand her ground. She dropped her backpack to the ground and put her arms by her sides in a nonchalant stance. She wanted to show disdain for the girl—not fear.

"What do you want to do now... bitch?" Bernadette said. She had her right foot poised. Ready to spring forward and kick her in the leg and follow with a quick shot to the nose. It was her best move.

The dark-haired girl closed on her. "You should know better—"

The next thing Bernadette knew, she was on the ground with the wind knocked out of her. The girl had punched her hard in the stomach.

"Didn't see that coming, did you, bitch," the dark-haired girl said. She turned to her gang. "See, that's what I wanted to talk to her about."

"Way to go, Susie, you taught her," a boy from the group laughed.

Bernadette lay on her side, her hands clutched to her stomach. The gang moved in on her. A boot landed on her back. She cried out in pain.

"All right. Back away now."

"Ah, shit, it's the cop, let's roll," Susie said.

A shadow came over Bernadette. "You can get up now."

Bernadette looked up to see a policewoman standing over her, extending her hand. She got up on her own. Being saved by the police was bad enough; having one help her up looked even worse.

"Thanks," Bernadette said. "I could have handled myself..."

"Yeah, you had them where you wanted them. I'm was waiting for you to leap up all ninja style and take them out," the policewoman said.

Bernadette dusted herself off, smiled at the policewoman. She was a little taller than her, with sandy blonde hair and bright blue eyes. There was a presence to her, though whether it was her physique or attitude, Bernadette couldn't tell, but it gave off a *don't mess with me* kind of vibe.

"Thanks," Bernadette said. "I guess I bit off a more than I could chew with them."

"Oh, yeah, just a little. My name's Constable Linda Myers... and you are?"

"Bernadette Callahan."

"You new here? Don't think I've seen you before."

"Just arrived today. I came to live with my aunt Mary and attend high school here. I'm from Lone Pine Reservation School near Fort Vermilion. Nobody's ever heard of it, it's kind of close to High Level... but then some people have never heard of that place either..." Bernadette said. She didn't know why she gave the officer all this information. Maybe it was the stress from the fight or she needed someone to talk to.

"Sure, I know Fort Vermilion. I was on a canoe trip up there, fishing for Arctic Grayling and Northern Pike. It's beautiful country," Myers said.

Bernadette stood there for a moment and realized how awkward it was for her to be talking to a policewoman. Other kids were stopping and watching. Across the street, in their cars, they were all watching her. Was she about to make a complaint? What was she doing talking to a cop?

"I gotta go... thanks for the help," Bernadette said.

"You're welcome," Constable Myers said. She looked around; she could see the other kids watching and knew she had little time with Bernadette. "Look, you need to know something. Those kids will come after you again."

"So. I can handle myself."

"Not from what I saw."

"Next time I'll know better. I'll defend myself better."

Constable Myers shook her head. "I hope you got something better in your repertoire than boots... if you lose the boots and change your clothes, they might leave you alone."

"Whaddya mean?"

"Here's the deal, they're a gang. They all dress in big black boots and black pants and jean jackets. To them you're wearing their uniform. You either join them or they beat you until you change what you're wearing," Constable Myers said.

"You think I should play chicken. I should run?" Bernadette asked.

"No, it's not chicken, it's called being smart. No one ever said to wave a red cape at a bull that wasn't in the ring. Why not give your bad girl look a rest? Come to school in some running shoes and jeans," Myers said. She looked in the direction the gang was walking. "Then you can outrun them. The way they smoke, you'd outdistance them in the first fifty metres."

"Thanks for the advice," Bernadette said. She turned and walked away. She didn't walk fast. There was a pace she needed, it showed she was leaving but at her own speed, still unbroken, not beaten. There would be another day. She knew it would be soon.

7

BERNADETTE MET her two cousins outside their school. They rushed up to meet her and gave her a hug.

"Did you learn anything today?" Abigail asked.

Bernadette's hand stroked her stomach. "Yeah, I learned a few things."

"I learned about elephants and tigers," Amber chimed in.

"Which do you like more?" Bernadette said.

Amber's face went into a scowl of concentration. "Elephants. They're kind and don't eat anybody." Her voice went into a whisper. "Did you know tigers are afraid of elephants?"

Bernadette took them by the hand. "No, Amber, I didn't know that." She imagined herself being an imposing elephant the next time she met Susie. Maybe she could learn to trumpet? She laughed at the thought and listened to the girl's chatter as they walked home.

There was soccer practice for both the girls. She fixed them a snack of bread and peanut butter, got them to change their clothes, and walked them back to the playing field a few blocks from the apartment.

She watched the girls run around with the others, trying to advance the soccer ball to the goal line. It seemed almost impossible as the girls went after the ball in a group instead of playing positions and passing the ball.

The coaches and parents yelled out instructions from the sidelines, which seemed to fall on deaf ears. The girls were in a life-and-death struggle for this brown object that wasn't bending to the will of their small feet.

Bernadette had brought a math book with her to study before class tomorrow. She leafed through the book to discover her new class would be more advanced than her previous one.

Her math skills were not great. She was a rote memory phenomenon, picking up and regurgitating dates in history, periodic tables in chemistry, or even verbs in French. But math was going to be a problem.

She looked up now and again to see the soccer game's progress. Nothing much had happened. The huddle of girls had moved from the middle of the field to twenty yards from the goal. The goalie was running from side to side in case a ball should, by a miracle, come hurling out of the mass. It didn't happen. The girls moved back towards centre field.

She noticed some bigger kids walking along the fence on the other side of the field. They were all dressed in black jeans, t-shirts, and denim jackets. Was this Susie's group?

Bernadette realized she was still in the same outfit she'd worn to school. She hadn't thought to change when she went home. Did they see her?

She closed her book and put it in her backpack. Looking around, she saw a group of adults sitting in the bleachers. Walking as slowly as she could with her knees quaking, she took a place behind the adults.

When she opened her book again, she saw the group. They come closer and stopped. Susie was pointing at her. They raised their middle fingers to her in a unified salute and walked away.

An older man in the group looked around at Bernadette. "I got a feeling the gesture was for you. Are you going to be okay on your way home?"

Bernadette smiled. "Thanks, but I'll be fine. They're just fooling around."

Her mouth was dry. Nausea formed in the pit of her stomach. This gang was becoming a problem. Were they out looking for her, or did they just stumble upon her in their rambling around the neighborhood?

Her cousins finished their soccer game and came over to her, all hot, flushed, and brimming with excitement. They exclaimed how many times they'd kicked the ball and the almost goals if someone had been there to kick it in.

They walked back home. Bernadette kept looking over her shoulder to see if a group dressed in black was following her. Instead of going straight home, she asked the girls if there was a sport store nearby.

"You mean, like sells soccer balls and stuff?" Abigail asked.

"Yeah, but also running shoes, Abigail. I need to get ready for gym class in a few days," Bernadette said.

"It's on the busy main street," Amber said. "We can't go there unless we're with Mom."

"You're with me now. Is it far?"

"No, but we'll miss our cartoon show," Abigail said. A frown appeared on her face. It was obvious Bernadette was crowding a much-loved show.

"Is there an ice cream store near the sports store?" Bernadette asked.

"Yeah. There's a Baskin Robbins on the corner, but Mom doesn't want us to eat it all the time, because she says it rots our teeth and it's not good for our tummies," Abigail said.

Bernadette stopped and looked down at the two girls. "We won't tell your mom now, will we?"

They broke into wide grins, and they skipped as they continued to the sports store; with ice cream in their near future—they forgot the cartoons.

Bernadette found a good pair of running shoes the store clerk assured her would have a good grip on any surface. She did not know what terrain she'd be escaping the gang from, but the shoes looked good. She picked up some gym socks and shorts to complete her purchase.

The girls had just about reached their attention limit by the time she finished. They licked happily on their ice cream cones as they made their way home.

Bernadette fixed the girls some soup and crackers. It was hard for them to finish with the walnut maple and vanilla strawberry ice cream still gurgling in their stomachs.

Somehow Bernadette got them into bed. She turned on the television and watched a *Beverly Hills 90210* rerun while munching popcorn. A new episode of *NYPD Blue* came on. She sat up with interest. Jimmy Smits was hot—she imagined him as a hot Latino love interest, doing things to her youthful body. The thoughts made her grow hot and uncomfortable.

A gunfight between Smits and a bad guy was on the screen with Smits getting the better of the bad guy. The bad guys always got it on *NYPD Blue*. It was typical, but who cared? It was mindless entertainment, and Smits was easy on the eyes.

She watched how Smits fought on the show. She thought about it as she made her bed on the couch and went to bed. There was a way he presented his body to the target. It gave her an idea for the next day.

8

AUNT MARY WAS STILL SNORING when Bernadette got the girls out of bed to get them breakfast and ready for school. She'd accepted her role now as the surrogate parent in this household.

She liked the girls. They had an easy way about them, and Aunt Mary—well, she was going to take some getting used to. There was a tension Bernadette felt around her, and she knew she wasn't a blessing being dropped on them, but it wasn't bad either as Aunt Mary could earn more money now.

Bernadette placed cereal and toast on the little kitchen table for the girls and made herself her usual toast and tea. She heard some movement from the bedroom, and Aunt Mary stood in the doorway.

"Did we wake you? Sorry, I was trying to keep the girls as quiet as possible," Bernadette said.

Aunt Mary walked over and tussled Amber's hair. "Hard to keep these two chatterboxes on low volume." She kissed Abigail on the forehead and made herself some tea. "How was your first day at school, you make any friends?"

Bernadette gulped her tea and almost choked on it. "Well, not exactly, I met a few people."

Aunt Mary stirred her tea and looked down at Bernadette. "You need to be careful whom you make friends with there. The school has a reputation for being tough. I'm hoping to move us to a nicer place once I get some money ahead, then get a better job."

Bernadette chewed on her toast and watched her aunt Mary collapse in the kitchen chair. She looked exhausted.

"How was the tavern last night?"

"Pretty packed. I was busy all night. The people in this neighborhood sure can drink, and they're not bad with tips either. I made over a hundred bucks last night. Took me an entire week to make that kind of money working days," Aunt Mary said.

Bernadette nodded her head and drank her tea. "I have some extra money I can put towards food." She took a twenty from her pocket and pushed it towards Aunt Mary. She sensed a need to ease Aunt Mary's burden of having her there.

"What're you going to do about school books and supplies?" Aunt Mary asked.

"Already bought them. I had some extra cash from a part-time job I had up north," Bernadette said. She didn't want to mention what the job was—it was fleecing the town kids in poker games on a weekly basis.

Aunt Mary stared at the twenty. She let it sit there and sipped her tea. "You getting along well with the girls?"

Bernadette smiled. "We're doing fine, aren't we, girls?"

Abigail beamed back at Bernadette, "Yeah, mom, Bernadette took us out to..." She stopped when she noticed Bernadette's frown.

Aunt Mary looked from the girls to Bernadette; she could see there was a conspiracy, and it involved ice cream or candy. "Just go easy on the sweets with these two. I haven't got extra money for dentist bills."

Bernadette nodded as she got up to get her things to go to school. She put on her denim jeans, a white t-shirt with a hooded sweatshirt and runners.

"You not wearing your kickin' boots today?" Aunt Mary asked.

"Ah... no." Bernadette said. "They make my feet sweat when I'm sitting in class all day."

"Good, those boots would be just asking for trouble at your school."

"Yeah, you're right, thanks for pointing that out," Bernadette said, slinging her backpack over her back.

Abigail and Amber wiped their mouths, gave their mom smeary peanut butter and jam kisses, and followed Bernadette out the door.

Bernadette dropped her cousins at their school, adjusted her backpack. With head down, she made determined strides to school.

She felt more incognito, like she'd fit in with students this time. No more waving her black boots and battle gear, there was a sense of contentment in her like this time she would just fit in and get along with the other students..

The feeling lasted until she heard the words, "Hey, bitch."

Her head snapped up to see Susie leaning against the fence. Her crew was there as well. They'd been waiting for Bernadette. It was obvious in their smiles, her arrival was their morning's highlight.

Bernadette slowed in her tracks. Susie approached her with a swagger, showing her crew she was in control of this young plaything she'd found.

"We saw you on the soccer field last night, you were wearing our colours. Why you doin' that when I gave you a beat down? Didn't you get the message I gave you? You need another one?"

"No, I think I'm good. I didn't have time to go home and change," Bernadette said.

Susie looked back at her crew. She wondered if this explanation from Bernadette was sufficient. They shook their heads in mock disbelief at Bernadette's lack of respect.

"Huh," Susie snorted, then spit on the ground. "You think you'd a had the time to change, when I said you were disrespecting us."

Bernadette shook her head. "I told you I didn't know you had a code, or dress code, or whatever..." She motioned down to her feet. "See, I changed my shoes, I changed my jeans, t-shirt, and my jacket. I'm no longer dressed like you, so why don't we call it lesson learned and I get to class."

The crew behind Susie let out a howl of laughter. One yelled, "Oh, Susie, she's sassing you now. The little bitch giving you lip."

"Is that it, you think you can talk your way out of another beating from disrespecting me?" Susie asked. She was balling her fist, marching towards Bernadette.

Bernadette dropped her backpack and turned sideways. She stared at Susie over her left shoulder, with her fist clenched, ready to land a knockout punch to Susie's chin.

Susie's fist landed on Bernadette's back. A sharp pain shot through her spine. She crumpled to the ground.

"Damn, she's stupid. She didn't see it coming neither," Susie yelled to her crew. "It's almost like beating up a baby, she's so stupid."

"Hey, cop's coming," a gang member said.

Constable Myers stood overhead. "Bernadette, you need to give up this fighting, you're not good at it. This is the second shit-kicking I've seen you take. You might wear Susie out, but at this rate you won't make it to Christmas."

Bernadette rolled over and got up. "God, the girl can punch."

"The crazy stance—why'd you do it?" Myers asked.

"I saw Jimmy Smits do it on *NYPD Blue* last night," Bernadette said, trying to gain her normal breathing.

"Oh god, it's a cop pose for holding a weapon. You don't do it in a fight. When you stand to the side, you give up two of your weapons, which is your left hand and left foot. Nobody does it in combat," Myers said.

"What are you talking about, this isn't combat—it's kids fighting," Bernadette said.

"You know what, you're just going to get your ass kicked until you learn some skills. It's obvious you want to keep standing up to those kids, so take this card," Myers said as she handed Bernadette a business card.

"I will not call you every time I get a beating."

"Nope, not my number, it's the address of a dojo."

"A do—what?"

"A dojo, a martial arts school. I train there three times a week. I'm going to get you three free lessons."

"I don't think I need it."

"From where I stand, you do... but if you don't want to come to the martial arts school, you need to take one piece of advice."

"What's that?"

"Take the long way around to school in the morning and afternoon. If you make a right before the school and run through the track field, you'll miss Susie and her gang. They think this is their turf —avoid it."

Bernadette picked up her backpack. "Thanks for the advice." She could feel the pain in her back and tried her best not to show how injured she was as she continued to school.

She eyed the long track field and wondered how much longer it would take her to get to school. Tomorrow she was going to try it.

9

"PICK UP THE PACE, Callahan, you're lagging," Coach Boz screamed from the sidelines.

Bernadette pushed harder. Her legs felt like lead. Her breathing felt wrong. She'd been taught a slow, steady rhythm in the long distance running. Gasping for breath was for sprinters.

It had been almost four weeks since Coach Boz, short for Bozniak, had noticed Bernadette run across his track each morning and afternoon. He'd approached her and asked her to join his track team. She'd agreed. Long distance runs with a group of girls her age seemed like fun. It'd had been until this past week.

"Callahan, close the gap, you're losing your team," Coach Boz screamed again.

Her group moved away from her. She was being dropped, the worst fear of any distance runner. The distance was eight laps around the four-hundred-metre track.

Bernadette had been building up to this for two weeks. She had always been in the lead, usually way ahead by a hundred metres. But not today—the past three days had been troubling her.

"Come on, Bernadette, you can do it, you can catch up," Melinda Cooper yelled from the sidelines as she passed. Melinda wasn't on the track team. She cheered the girl's track team and been Bernadette's number one fan.

Bernadette had befriended Melinda to ask for her help in math class. The kid was a total geek who excelled in math and sucked at meeting people. She helped Bernadette understand math, and in hanging with her, she met people. Bernadette called it a symbiotic friendship. And Bernadette liked the girl.

Melinda's words made her push herself. She gained a few metres on the group and then fell behind again. Her dreams bothered her, that and her aunt's strange behavior.

The strange dreams had begun with ravens flying overhead. Ravens were good omens to native people. How would they be a problem? They'd sent a chill, and she'd wake shivering. And then the wolves appeared. She'd heard them howling. They sounded so real she'd wake at night to peek outside the window.

The dreams disturbed her—but her aunt bringing men home disturbed her even more. Her aunt and some big man, both reeking of beer, would shake her awake and tell her to sleep in the other room. The lovemaking sounds would keep her awake until her aunt's companion would leave an hour or two later.

The combination unravelled Bernadette. She'd held on for as long as possible. Her stride slowed. Lack of sleep and worry drained her energy.

"You got a piano tied to your butt, Callahan," Coach Boz yelled as she passed on the fifth lap. "There's twelve hundred metres left, when you going to make a move?"

Fatigue hit her. She wanted to stop running, lie down beside the track, and let the earth fold over her. Her eyes gazed at soft grass. If she just stopped... all the pain would be over.

But she wasn't a quitter—she would finish. She relaxed her breathing by drawing a breath deep into her abdomen and letting it all the way out. Much better. Deeper breathing meant more oxygen to the blood.

Her pace improved to two hundred metres behind the group—

she was gaining ground. Was there enough track left in the race to make it happen?

She got lost in her thoughts again. Could she lose her aunt to alcohol like she'd lost her dad? How would she look after the girls? Could she take them back to the reservation? No, not an option. She wouldn't be welcome there—too dangerous for her and for them.

The bell rang. One lap left to go. She broke from her thoughts. She looked up. The group got farther ahead. She picked up speed, almost to a sprint; she closed, but the group picked up speed as well. They raced for positions now.

Coach Boz screamed for her to run, echoed by Melinda. They sounded far away. Suddenly she burst into the present. She crossed the finish line twenty metres behind the other girls.

Melinda handed Bernadette a towel. "Good try, Bernadette. You'd have closed on them if you'd had more time."

"More time? My god, the girl had three kilometres to close in. What happened out there, Callahan?" Coach Boz asked. He stood there, clipboard in hand, dressed in grey sweats with his whistle and stop watch hanging around his neck.

Bernadette looked up at Coach Boz. "Sorry, Coach, it's a case of wrong anatomy—you know—head up my butt."

"And what have I told you to do when it happens?"

"Windex my navel and keep running?"

"Exactly," Coach Boz replied with a smile. The girls on the team adored him. He was mid-forties, stocky with a paunch showing his competitive days were over, but he knew the sport inside and out.

"Don't worry, Bernadette, you'll do better next time," Melinda said.

"Can you give us a minute, Melinda?" Coach asked.

"Sure," Melinda said. She wandered away at an amble to display her feelings of being left out.

"Anything going on, Bernadette?"

"What'd you mean?"

"As in at home or your schoolwork?"

Bernadette bent down like she needed to catch her breath. She didn't want to meet the coach's gaze. A tear formed in her eye. She didn't know why. "No, Coach, I'm fine. Just a bad day, I guess."

"I've seen you outrun everyone in the past few weeks. I make you for a world-class distance runner. You'd get a scholarship if you ran at the pace you did last week."

Bernadette wiped her face with her towel and stood up. "Yeah, coach, you said that last week."

"Don't you want to go to university? I'd have scouts from universities in Canada and the United States for next year's spring meet if you'd maintain your pace."

Bernadette shook her head. "I do not know what I want to do yet, Coach." She ran the towel over her head. "Look, I'll clean up my act, I'll get my head out of my butt and run hard for you and the team —okay?"

"Go run a few recovery laps. Get your head aligned and think about your future," the coach said. He walked away, peering down at his clipboard and wondering if his track star would keep fading.

Bernadette threw her towel aside and started running around the track. She began at an easy pace and then picked it up slightly. Coach Boz's words were echoing in her head. University had never crossed her mind. Hell, she'd never thought beyond high school.

Any job paying above minimum wage would be fine. She didn't want to end up slinging beer in some dive like her aunt. She'd drive a truck or dig ditches to get away from office work and be outside.

The first lap was easy. She settled into a steady pace and thought about whether she should call her grandma. Perhaps Grandma Moses would interpret Bernadette's dreams, and if she came to the city, she might deal with Aunt Mary too. Grandma Moses had a special way with people. She saw into their hearts and minds.

The last lap became easier. She'd run halfway round the track when she saw some figures in black by the bleachers. *Was it Susie and her gang?*

The next lap would have her by the bleachers. She cut across the track field and headed for the showers. Her meetings with Susie had never gone well. Avoidance had become her best strategy.

In the locker rooms, she looked around. No one followed her. She sighed, instantly feeling relieved and safe. She peeled off her running gear and turned the shower on and stepped in.

Bernadette let the water run down her back to loosen the muscles in her legs. She appreciated the individual school shower with their privacy curtains. She lingered in them as long as she wanted.

At home, Abigail and Amber pounded on the door, wanting to get in, or asking her for something. This became as close to her own sanctuary as she'd ever find.

The other girls had left. They'd given her reassuring words, then disappeared. Their incessant chatter echoed down the hallway until there was just the sound of water and Bernadette. Pure bliss.

The shower room door opened. Boots sounded on the tiled floor. Bernadette held her breath. She turned off the shower.

"Hey there, Bernadette, don't worry, just us girls come to pay a visit." It was Susie's voice.

"Yeah, come to pay respects to the track star," another female voice said.

Bernadette's body shook. She breathed in deeply. *Don't show fear,* she told herself. She pulled open the shower curtain. "Thanks for the visit, girls, but I got to get home now." She reached for her towel from outside the shower—Susie grabbed it.

"Not cool, girls. Gimme the towel and I won't tell Coach Bozniak you were in here, okay?" Bernadette said with as much feigned authority as she could muster.

"You going to tell on us, little girl? That's what you going to do?" Susie asked. She came closer to Bernadette.

Bernadette shielded her body as best she could with her arms.

"Cute bod you got there, girl," one girl said. She was tall, tightly encased in a black t-shirt and pants bulging with her excess fat. She didn't seem happy Bernadette was so fit. It was sarcasm, not a compliment.

"Look, this isn't funny; give me my towel back, now," Bernadette said. She was over being scared, she was angry. They'd invaded her space, her sanctuary.

Susie dangled the towel just beyond her reach, "go on—take it."

Alarm bells rang in Bernadette's head. If she waited them out, maybe the janitors or another student would come by, and they would defuse this in a minute. But the towel, it was a red flag as it would be to a bull.

She jumped from the shower and grabbed the towel with one hand and landed a punch to Susie's head with the other. Susie went down on the floor.

"Now you've done it," the big girl said.

Susie rolled over on the floor, slipping several times before she got up. She was wet and mad. She came at Bernadette with fists raised. The other two girls joined in.

Bernadette didn't remember when she blacked out. The blows seemed to last forever. Susie's fury had no bounds. She heard the words, "Stop, Susie, you might kill her. Stop—"

10

A LIGHT APPEARED ABOVE BERNADETTE, it looked on the surface. Was she under water? She couldn't see her hands.

She lifted her arms and propelled herself upwards; as she rose, the water became warmer. She hit the surface, coming into light. Her eyes opened. She woke up in a hospital room.

Long cords attached to Bernadette under her covers, running back to the machine beside her that beeped away in a rhythm showing her vitals as stable. She took it as a good sign.

Grandma Moses occupied an armchair beside the bed, her breath going in and out in a soft snore. Bernadette had gone to sleep for so many years to her grandma's snoring; she'd missed it when moving to the city. She looked at her grandma, her heart filled with tenderness for her.

Her grandma snorted and woke up. "Ah, you're awake finally."

Bernadette spoke in a raspy voice. "How long have I been asleep?"

"Three days."

"Oh my god, I missed two exams!"

"Don't worry, you've had all your teachers and school kids in here to check on you. They'll let you do the exams later. How you feeling?"

Grandma Moses asked, sitting up in the chair and taking Bernadette's hand.

"Like I got hit by a stampede. Am I badly injured?"

Grandma Moses massaged her hand. "Not bad. You have a stress fracture in your right leg, a concussion, and a lot of bruises. A doctor came in here. He said you would heal in a few months if you rest."

"A few months. I'll miss the indoor track event next month."

Grandma Moses shrugged. "But you'll heal. You can run another time."

Bernadette's eyes filled with tears. "There is no other time. The track event would have gotten me into the finals for the year. It was a springboard to a scholarship."

"You're alive, Bernadette. That matters. Whoever attacked you came close to giving you a massive concussion. Are you going to tell the police who did this?"

"The police. Are they involved in this?"

"The janitors found you unconscious in the shower. The police have been here. They want you to say who did this," Grandma Moses said. She gave Bernadette a plastic water cup with a straw and watched as Bernadette drained it.

Bernadette put her hand to her head. Her other hand had an intravenous line with a drip from a bag. She was realizing how badly the girls had beaten her.

"But... Grandma, I started it... I struck the other girl first. I pissed her off, and she went nuts on me," Bernadette said.

"A fight is one thing, trying to kill you is another," Grandma Moses said. She got up slowly and poured more water in the cup for Bernadette.

"When did you get here?" Bernadette asked, trying to change the subject.

"Mary phoned me the evening they found you. The school called her at work. I started driving the moment I got the phone call."

"You drove the seven hours from Lone Pines at night," Bernadette said. She sipped more water from the cup—her grandma's stamina amazed her.

Grandma Moses let a small smile edge her lips. "You take it one hour at a time."

"I have a question to ask you, Grandma."

"What is it?"

"I've dreamed of ravens and black wolves in the past week. What does it mean?" Bernadette asked.

Grandma Moses sat down, staring into Bernadette's eyes. "Ravens are a good omen to our people. They are smart and teach us things. Wolves are also a noble brother to our people, but you saw black wolves?"

Bernadette stared out the hospital window. "Yes... many black wolves. They howled so much in my dreams I thought they were outside the window."

Grandma Moses squeezed Bernadette's hand. "There are always two wolves inside you. A white one and a black one: the white one is good and does no harm. He lives in harmony with all around him and does not take offense when no offense is intended. He will only fight when it is right to do so, and in the right way."

"But the black wolf is full of anger. The smallest thing will set him off. He fights everyone, all the time. He cannot think because his anger is so great. It is helpless anger, for anger will change nothing. It is hard to live with these two wolves inside you, for both seek to dominate your spirit."

Bernadette looked at her grandma. "Which one wins, Grandma?"

"The one you feed. Now, get some sleep," Grandma Moses said.

Bernadette's eyes became heavy. They closed on their own, like lead weights dropping. She dreamed. Large snowflakes fell. A white wolf appeared beside her.

Her hand brushed its warm fur. They walked together, descending a steep incline into a valley layered with snow. She looked up to the valley ridge and saw black shapes.

Black wolves ringed the valley. They howled, a long rising wail echoed in the hills. She wasn't afraid. Her right hand dug deeper in the white wolves' fur as they walked.

She woke up to daylight outside the window. Big flakes of snow were falling. A nurse stood over her, smiling. "Good to have you with us, Bernadette, I'm Nurse Marcia. I'm on days, and I'll be unhooking you from these wonderful contraptions they have attached you to."

Nurse Marcia looked Asian, maybe Filipino. She'd met a few Filipinos. They spoke with a singsong voice, like they wanted to continue their sentence on a high note.

"I'm going to take your catheter out now, okay," Nurse Marcia said with a smile, making it sound like it would be a mild inconvenience. As the device came out, Bernadette had an unusual sensation.

"Wow, kind of weird," Bernadette said.

"It's okay, it's out now, we'll be taking you to the bathroom from now on so you can go potty all on your own," Marcia said.

Bernadette frowned at the word "potty." Hold old this nurse think she was, three? She watched as the nurse pulled out the IV, then unhooked a heart rate monitor from her chest.

When the nurse finished, she felt lighter. She wondered what day it was. The track event had been on Friday. Grandma Moses said she'd been out for three days. She figured it must be Monday or Tuesday.

The smell of food wafted into the room. A large metal cabinet loaded with trays appeared in the outside hallway. Breakfast appeared before her. She removed the plastic cover to find semi-warm oatmeal sprinkled with brown sugar. The food looked horrible. But then, all hospital food was. She poured some milk on the oatmeal and dug in. Her stomach would have to get over the awful food.

She was sipping on her tepid tea when a policewoman in a uniform filled her doorway. Her oatmeal did a flip in her stomach. She'd dreaded this moment.

"Hi, Bernadette, I heard you woke up. I'm glad you're feeling better," Officer Linda Myers said.

Bernadette sat upright in bed. "Yeah, the doctors said I'll be out of here in a few days. Guess I can take a licking and keep on ticking." She made a small laugh at her Timex watch joke.

"I read the doctor's report," Myers said. "They came close to causing you some pretty serious injuries. You're lucky they found you in time."

Bernadette sniffed and pulled a tissue from the beside table. "Well, yeah, I'm a lucky girl." She blew her nose softly and dropped the tissue on her side table.

Officer Myers sat in the chair; she didn't want to stand and make this an interrogation. She needed Bernadette to open up to her, and she could see the hesitation. "Do you want to tell me who did this to you?"

Bernadette looked out the window. "No, I don't."

"Why not?"

"Because I started it."

Myers leaned forward, "It doesn't matter who started this. You were naked in the shower. We found three sets of boot prints in there. Even if you took a swing at Susie and her gang, they had no reason to beat you so violently."

"I didn't say it was Susie," Bernadette said. Her face turned red with the stress she felt from Myer's questions.

Myers shook her head. "We know it was Susie Ferguson and her gang. I just need you to give me a description of the other girls and a statement."

Bernadette lowered her head. "I have too much black wolf inside me. It was my fault."

"I do not know what you're talking about. If this is a native shaman thing, fine, but in the meantime I want to put Susie and her petty thugs into juvenile detention," Myers said.

"Susie would go to prison... if I ID'd her?"

"In a heartbeat," Myers said. "She has a string of priors. She's attending school on strict probation. The assault on you, will put her back in juvenile detention. She won't be out until she turns eighteen."

Bernadette pursed her lips. "No, I do not know who attacked me in the shower. My memory is blank. Sorry, I have nothing for you."

"I hate to say it, but it's your funeral, kid. Girls like Susie count on you to roll over and play dead. She'll keep pushing her luck until she hurts or kills someone. I just hope it's not you," Myers said as she got up.

Myers left the room. A veil of sadness fall over her. What was she going to do? She watched the snow falling outside. The flakes were getting bigger.

11

BERNADETTE CAME BACK HOME to the apartment on Friday. Her aunt couldn't hide her disappointment—the tirade began the moment she got in the door. "Didn't I tell you it's a tough school? Didn't I tell you to stay away from fights? Look what you've done. Your grandma had to drive down to care for you. Don't you see I got two kids of my own? You think this is easy what I'm doing here?"

Bernadette walked with her cane to the sofa. She had to use it for a few weeks until the stress fracture healed. Her foot was in a brace; she took it off at night and put on a special sock.

Abigail and Amber crowded around her and gave her hugs. "We're glad you're home," Abigail said. "We didn't like the hospital—it smelled bad."

"Yeah, it was pretty bad. I didn't like it either. Who's been taking you to school while I was away?" Bernadette asked.

"I did, if you want to know—I had to get up after a few hours' sleep and take them, then go back to bed," Aunt Mary said as she polished the kitchen table in violent swipes. The table shook, spoons jumped, clattering to the floor.

Bernadette bit her lip; it was a dumb question to ask. "Sorry..."

she said meekly. "I'll take over on Monday. The doctor said I could walk, just no running. So... no problem."

"You're damn right it's no problem, you'll be pulling your weight around here, and fast," Aunt Mary said. She finished in the kitchen and stomped off to the bedroom.

"Mom's mad at you," Amber said.

"Yep, I get that, thanks, Amber." Bernadette said. She picked up her schoolbooks and looked at the homework Melinda had dropped off. There'd be Math, English, and French tests on Monday. She needed to study and complete some assignments.

Aunt Mary left for work at four. Her scowl lingered in the apartment long after she'd left. If Grandma Moses had stayed another few days, things might have been smoother. That wasn't an option with the cramped quarters of the apartment.

Bernadette made the kids beans and franks with a salad for dinner. Then got them to do their homework, which was identifying the dinosaurs that ate other dinosaurs and which one's ate plants, and plunked them in front of the television while she did her homework with her headphones on. At nine thirty she put them to bed and fell asleep on the sofa.

She was into a dreamless sleep when she heard the apartment door open. Her aunt came in. She wasn't alone.

Her aunt was giggling and whispering to a man who was asking in a gruff voice why he needed to keep quiet.

"'Cause you'll wake my kids, you dummy," Aunt Mary answered in a slurred voice.

Bernadette didn't wait for Aunt Mary to tell her to go to the other room. She grabbed her cane and limped as quietly as she could into the bedroom and closed the door.

The sounds of lovemaking began almost immediately. The man was talking loudly. Aunt Mary kept telling him in hushed whispers to keep quiet.

There was a loud slap. A yell of "no." Bernadette bolted out of bed. She grabbed the cane and rushed into the room. Aunt Mary was standing; she had only her panties on, with her hand on her cheek. She looked frightened.

Bernadette turned on the lights. "I think you'd better leave."

"Bullshit. I'm showing Mary how to have rough sex—she'll learn to love it. How about we do a threesome? I got enough juice for the both of you," the man said. He was weaving as he stood there. "Mary, you didn't tell me you had a tasty little daughter."

"She's not my daughter, she's my niece, and she's sixteen."

"I've cracked a few virgins in my time, happy to do it for her."

"You're not cracking anyone, mister. Get out, now," Bernadette said. Her breath came in quick gasps. Her hands were shaking.

"You gonna make me, little girl?"

Bernadette thought about it for a second. This guy was big and drunk. She had a cane. That wouldn't do much. There was a carving knife in the kitchen. She could slice his leg and maybe hit his femoral artery, then let the bastard bleed to death. She needed another option.

"No, here's what I'm going to do." Bernadette walked to the hallway door. "I'm going to open this door and start screaming help— police—rape at the top of my lungs. There's several people in this building who work nights just like my aunt—they're home."

"Bullshit, you not going to—"

Bernadette opened the door. "Last chance. You leave or I scream. You look like a guy whose had a few brushes with the law; feel lucky?"

"Bitch."

"I get that a lot, mister, now start walking," Bernadette said.

The man walked by Bernadette. She could feel the heat from his body as he brushed by. He made like he wanted to strike her, but she shook her head. "Don't try it."

She slammed the door, locked it, and put the chain on before collapsing on the floor.

Aunt Mary threw on her t-shirt and came to Bernadette's side. "I'm sorry, kid, it was stupid to bring him here." She put her head in her hands, and low sobs came.

Bernadette looked up at her aunt. "You want to tell me what's going on here? What's with you bringing a big offensive drunk home? I'm not supposed to get into fights, but this the dumbest thing I've ever seen."

Aunt Mary sobbed quietly; a muffled "I know," came from her hands.

Bernadette got up from the floor and guided Aunt Mary to the kitchen table and put on some tea. The bedroom door opened. The two little faces of the girls appeared.

"Go back to bed, girls," Bernadette said.

"We're scared," Abigail said. "We heard loud voices."

"Loud voices—like monsters," Amber said.

"We had the TV turned too loud, sorry," Bernadette said.

"Is mommy okay?" Amber asked.

"Your mommy's fine, the television scared her too, now go back to bed."

The girls closed the door slowly after peering around the corner to see if any new monsters had appeared.

Bernadette made tea, placed two mugs on the table with the milk and sugar. She stirred her tea and looked at her aunt. "I need to know, and I'm going to ask you directly, are you having a problem with alcohol? Because if you are, I'll take care of your kids while you go to rehab."

Aunt Mary shook her head, "No, it's not the alcohol I'm having a problem with, it's you."

"Me? You want me to leave? I'm out of here—."

"No, it's not you, it's what you remind me of."

Bernadette stirred her tea and put her spoon down. "Okay, Aunt Mary, enough mystery, why don't you tell me what you mean?"

Aunt Mary sighed. "When you came here, it wasn't having an extra person here—you've been great with the kids, and they love you. You remind me of your mom."

"I thought you and my mom were tight once."

"Yeah, once..." Aunt Mary sniffed. She blew her nose in a Kleenex and looked at Bernadette through bleary eyes. "Long before your dad appeared on the scene, your mom and I sang together."

"Were you any good?"

"Good? Hell yeah, we were amazing," Aunt Mary said with a smile. "We sang here in Edmonton, did some gigs down in Calgary, and we had an agent who wanted us to go to Nashville."

"Nashville? You must have been great. What happened?"

Aunt Mary's face turned into a bitter frown. "Your father happened, the sweet-talking Dominic Callahan. He convinced your mom she was the star, and I just sang harmony in the group."

"I'm sorry about my dad... I didn't know."

Aunt Mary stirred her tea, then sighed. "No... there's more to it..."

"You want to tell me the complete story, 'cause I got all night," Bernadette said.

"Your mom and I both wanted your dad. We saw him up there on the stage one night and we were two love-struck girls."

"And he chose my mom?"

"Yeah, the whole thing about the voices came out—which one sang better with him and his band. I was the odd girl out. My solo singing career didn't pan out. So I began slinging beer as a server and having kids with men that didn't stick around," Aunt Mary said. She looked out the window. Bernadette saw a faraway look as if she'd seen her past slip away from her.

"I'm sorry it didn't turn out like you wanted, but then, I wonder how many times it happens... the broken dreams and all," Bernadette said.

"Happens all the time: we have hopes and dreams... and they get crushed." Aunt Mary put her hand on Bernadette's. "I'm sorry, kid, when you arrived here... I'd remembered my hopeless past and saw my dismal future. I've been drinking and dragging men home to drown out the feeling."

"Are you done now?" Bernadette asked. "'Cause it's been getting a little weird."

"Yeah, I'm done. No more crazy men coming into the place. I'm going to finish my shifts and come home man-less and sober."

"Wonderful, and I'm going to stay away from fighting. Especially since I haven't been wining any of them," Bernadette said.

They got up from the table and hugged, then went to bed. Bernadette went back to the sofa and felt as if someone had lifted a weight. She'd seen her father descend into alcoholism and didn't want to see her aunt Mary do the same.

One hurdle taken care of, now all she needed to do was go to school on Monday, walk by Susie and her gang without getting into any fights, and pass three exams. "Nothing like a challenge," she murmured to herself as she fell asleep.

12

MONDAY CAME with an early winter storm. An Arctic front descended with high winds and heavy snow. The temperature dropped all Sunday night. By Monday morning it was -15 Celsius with snow drifts pilling up on the ground. Bernadette looked out the apartment window and wondered how she was going to navigate the sidewalks with her walking splint and cane. She shook her head; she had to get to school.

The girls wore big parkas with scarves wrapped around their heads so many times there was only a slit from which they could see. They had on thick mitts and boots and stood in the hallway whining about how they were getting too hot and had to get outside.

Bernadette threw on her heavy down parka. She pulled on one boot; on her other foot, she pulled on four extra socks with a thick garbage bag and several elastic bands to keep her splint dry. It wasn't pretty, but it worked.

They walked in single file to school. Bernadette broke trail through the snow drifts until she dropped the girls off. Schools in the north closed at -23, and this was not even close, just damned cold.

Once the girls were safely inside their school, Bernadette made her way to hers. She got used to walking with the splint, sliding it forward like a ski in the snow.

She was making excellent progress. A small crowd of black appeared midway between the school boundary and the entrance. Bernadette sighed, shook her head.

Susie's gang was her welcoming committee. There was no way to go around. It was too late to cut through the running track. It was too deep in snow. There was no way back. She put her head down, concentrating on the steps in the deep snow.

"Well, look who it is," Susie said when Bernadette got close. "If it ain't the little scrapper." Susie detached herself from the group, huddling in the wind to keep warm. She stood in front of Bernadette.

"I'm not fighting you, Susie," Bernadette said. She moved her backpack to adjust its weight and stared at Susie.

"Yeah, 'cause you're tired of getting a beat down. I can't believe you didn't squeal to the cops."

"Because if I had, they said you'd be inside juvie hall until you were eighteen. Now, you want to step aside," Bernadette said.

"You think you scare me? I could beat the hell out of you right in front of the school, and do the time in a heartbeat, you hear me, you see I ain't scared?"

Bernadette stood facing Susie. There was nowhere to go but forward, to go through Susie to get to school. A loud crunch of footsteps sounded in the snow. A group of boys came running towards her.

"Hey, Bernadette," one boy yelled. It was Travis Archer, captain of the wrestling team. "We're glad you're back at school. Sorry we didn't see you sooner."

Travis brushed by Susie and put his arm around Bernadette and took her backpack. "I told Coach the wrestling team would be your chaperons to school from now on, sorry we got delayed with this morning's snow."

"Hey, I ain't done talking to her yet," Susie said. She crossed her arms and placed her legs in a wide stance to show she was serious.

"Yeah, you're done," Travis said.

"You think I can't bust you upside the head?" Susie asked, taking her hands down into a boxing stance.

"You can try," Travis smirked. "I'm the wresting team captain and province-wide boxing champion, if you want to take a shot at me. Susie, I'll put you in hospital far longer than you did Bernadette."

A chorus of cheers rose from the boys behind Susie's gang. One boy yelled, "How about if we put all of Susie's gang in hospital. Be our morning workout."

Bernadette put her hand up. "Okay, you guys, stop it. There's no need to fight. I'm going to class to write my exams and, Susie, I think you've probably got some classes as well."

Travis took Bernadette by the arm, and they walked through the gang. Susie and her crew muttered and swore at them as they passed.

"Thanks," Bernadette said as they got by them. "I wasn't sure what I was going to do. I was running out of options."

"Hey, you've got me, and my team, we got your back," Travis said. He was an easygoing guy, tall, handsome with blond hair and blue eyes. A guy Bernadette could see hanging with the most popular girls in school. She knew he was doing this because of Coach Boz.

"Well, thank you, and thank Coach Boz for thinking about me," Bernadette said.

"It was my idea actually, Bernadette," Travis said. He stood beside her. He was a full head taller at six foot five and had to look down at her. "It's my way of apologizing for not getting your back earlier. I saw Susie take you on when you first came to school, and I did nothing... I'm sorry."

"Oh... that's okay," Bernadette said as her face became red and her words got all flustered inside her head. "Thanks."

She rushed away as fast as she could, hobbling down the hallway towards her first class. Did Travis like her?

Her exams were a blur; she progressed from one class to another and completed each exam in record time. The answers came to her easily. She'd developed a knack for retaining facts at an early age.

When hunting with her grandfather back on the reservation, he'd always ask her to remember the trees and special features when they hiked on the trails. "What does that tree looks like to you?"

"It looks like a giant with its arms outstretched," Bernadette would say.

"Do you know where it is on the trail?"

"Yes, I do, Grandfather."

When they'd come back on the trail, her grandfather would ask her to call out the special features she remembered. She never lost her way in the forest, and her memory had become a force.

When her class ended, her homeroom teacher told her to go to the administration office to meet with Ms. Blacksburg. She did not know why but shuffled off wondering what additional trouble she might be in with the school.

The school counselor, Ms. Blacksburg, asked her to come inside her office and closed the door behind her. Bernadette walked into the office to see Officer Myers sitting there.

"Take a seat," Ms. Blacksburg said. It was a command, not an offer.

Bernadette sat down. "Am I in trouble?"

"No, it's not to do with you." Myers said. "But we've just heard Susie is threatening your friend, Melinda."

"What, why would she threaten Melinda?" Bernadette asked.

"So she can get at you," Myers said. "I told you in the hospital. Susie won't quit. She wants to show her dominance over you."

"What can I do?" Bernadette asked.

"We can get you into a downtown school," Ms. Blacksburg said. "Victoria Composite High has room. Your marks are excellent, and I can put in the transfer immediately. You can be there in two days' time."

"But I have my cousins to look after. If I took the bus, I couldn't take them or pick them up from school and make them dinner," Bernadette said. She began to breathe heavily. Having to give up the care of her little cousins threw her mind into a panic.

Myers looked from the counselor to Bernadette. "I understand the wrestling team is giving you an escort at school, which is great, but they can't protect you all the time, and neither can they protect Melinda."

Bernadette got up. "I'm not leaving my cousins, and I'm not going to another school to avoid that thug." She clenched her fists in defiance.

Ms. Blacksburg looked at Myers and shrugged, as if she'd known what Bernadette's answer would be.

Bernadette walked out of the office, and Myers followed her out. She turned and faced Myers. "Does the offer still stand for those Karate lessons?"

"In your condition?"

Bernadette threw her hands wide. "Look, my leg will get better; in the meantime, I can start work on some martial arts moves."

"You sure about this?"

"Yeah, I'm sure. Susie isn't going away until she's beaten me and my friends into the ground. I'm the one who can put an end to this."

13

Bernadette put her organizing skills to use. In order to protect Melinda, she had Travis put two members of the wrestling team with her at all times.

For Melinda's part, it thrilled her. Here she was, a geek being escorted by two burly boys in team jackets. She walked down the hall with one on each arm. Melinda dressed better and took care of her hair. By the end of the week, she was dating one of the good-looking boys.

Bernadette needed to get some extra money to help her aunt, maybe move to a bigger apartment. The sofa was okay, but not great. And she knew once her intro karate lessons were up, she would need to pay.

There wasn't just one but three poker games at school. She became a regular at all the games, making sure she didn't win all the time, but never lost much. She quietly won two to three hundred per week off her quarry.

She was always on the lookout for Susie, who so far wasn't making any appearances. Was she biding her time? Waiting for the wrestling team to disappear?

Bernadette had to confide in her aunt. There was no way she

could disappear off to karate class without taking the girls along three times a week. She'd need them to be in on her plan as well.

"You're going to do what?" Aunt Mary asked when Bernadette told her.

"I'm going to do karate, for self defense," Bernadette said.

"You will not use this to get in more fights?"

"No, I just want people to know I can handle myself, so they'll leave me alone."

"Hmm, will you teach me those moves later?" Aunt Mary asked with a smile and a hug.

That was the end of the conversation. Bernadette started karate school two weeks after her showdown with Susie.

The karate school was off a busy side street. Cars and trucks whizzed by, throwing slush on the sidewalk as Bernadette crossed the street with the two girls in tow. They were both excited to see this karate thing. Bernadette had shown them a video called *Rumble in the Bronx* with Jackie Chan.

The girls couldn't wait to see Bernadette do the same moves. How could she tell them those were stunt men doing those moves, and with multiple takes?

"Are you going to be Jackie Chan's sidekick?" Abigail asked.

"No," Bernadette said, glaring at a car not slowing down enough for them to cross the street. "I'm going to learn some basic skills, you know, to defend myself better."

Amber walked beside Bernadette, one hand holding on to Bernadette, the other making karate chops. "Karate chop, karate chop, karate chop," she repeated to some aggressors she could see in her mind.

They entered the karate school. It looked less appealing from the inside than it did on the outside. The place looked bleak. A sea of mats covered a well-worn hardwood floor. Japanese banners with odd-looking pictures of men covered the white walls.

Bernadette was mindful to take off her boots and those of the girls. Officer Myers had told her the protocols to follow when she entered. She'd been told she was entering a *dojo,* which literally meant "place of the way or training" in Japanese.

She took off her jacket and helped the girls hang theirs up on the wall. A tall young girl dressed in the white outfit with a green belt greeted them.

The girl bowed to Bernadette, putting her hands together, one fist cupped by the other hand. "Oss, I am Senpai Sarah. I was told by Linda you were coming."

Bernadette remembered from Linda she needed to respond in kind. "Oss," she said with a bow. "I am Bernadette, good to meet you."

Amber tugged Bernadette's sleeve. "Why are you hissing at each other? Why'd she call herself a sen...?"

Sarah laughed. "This is not hissing, young lady, this is a greeting karate students make to one another and to their instructor... and I'm called a senpai as I'm an advanced student."

Abigail whispered in Amber's ear. "It's like Jackie Chan."

"Oh... like Jackie Chan," Amber repeated in a whisper.

"Come with me," Sarah said. "I'll show you to the change room. Did you bring a gi?"

"Yes, I did," Bernadette said. She slung her gym bag over her shoulder and followed Sarah into a small change room. The gi she had purchased through a classified ad cost her twenty-five dollars, or one hand of poker drawing to an inside straight. Sarah showed her how to tie her belt correctly. The gi seemed weird at first. It was big at the top with wide arms, and the belt held it together. The bottom was wide as well and short. There were no shoes required. She was told all training sessions were to be in bare feet. A good thing, since she couldn't keep running up her poker winnings to purchase more equipment.

"You put the seam down, right over left, then left over right," Sarah said as she helped her with her belt. "You have a white belt, signifying a novice. Now, follow me."

Sarah led her out to join the other students. They lined up in a row as a short, balding man with wide shoulders walked into the room. He stood before them. A low bow from all the students followed a loud chorus of "Oss."

The man walked up to Bernadette. "I am Sensei David Krapinski. I assume you are my new student, Bernadette?"

Bernadette bowed. "Yes, sensei. It is nice to meet you and thank you for allowing me to train in your dojo."

Sensei returned the bow. "You're welcome. The karate style I teach is Goju. It is the way of the hard and soft." He put his open hand over his fist. "'Go,' meaning hard, and 'ju' meaning soft. In this class you will learn karate is a way of life. This is above and beyond the basic moves of self-defense."

Sensei moved closer and lowered his voice. "I understand you're injured. Do what you can in class. We run in our warm-ups: walk if you have any pain. I do not want you to injure yourself any more. Understand?"

"Yes... Oss, sensei," Bernadette said.

Sensei smiled. "I will give you a lot of instruction and information tonight. I don't expect you to learn the moves in one night. The more you come, the more the moves will become familiar."

Bernadette smiled back. "Oss, sensei."

Sensei called out to Sarah. "Senpai Sarah, lead the warm up."

"Oss, sensei," Sarah called back in a loud and affirmative voice. "Laps."

The class ran around the dojo, running on the balls of their feet. They mixed it up with side steps. Bernadette walked and limped around the room as best she could. She felt out of place. What was she doing here?

Sarah commanded the class to stop running. "Push-ups. On your fists."

Bernadette followed suit. Her knuckles screamed with pain.

Sensei kneeled beside her. In a quiet voice he said, "Keep your wrists straight and do them off your front two knuckles. Do as many as you can then change to regular push-ups. Twenty-five will be enough for now."

Senpai Sarah yelled out, "Sit-ups."

The class rolled on their backs and began furious stomach crunches. Bernadette wondered what the hell she'd got herself into. Her training was running. Sit-ups were a thing she did once in a while. When they hit the high twenties, her abs were singing a song of pain. When they hit the final fifty, her abs had turned to jelly.

Sensei split the class into belt levels. A senior belt or senpai led each group. Senpai Sarah was assisting Bernadette's white belt group.

"Bernadette, make a fist," Sarah said.

Bernadette threw up her standard fist with her thumb tucked alongside her index finger.

Senpai Sarah walked over to Bernadette, unfolding her thumb and tucking it underneath her knuckles. "You do this so you don't catch a thumb when striking with the fist. You see?" She placed Bernadette's fist in the correct posture. It instantly seemed tighter, more compact.

"These moves are *Katas*. You will repeat them until you learn how to stand, walk and move in balance." Sarah said.

Sensei walked among the students, correcting postures and giving words of encouragement.

After an hour mark, there was a water break. Beads of sweat were running down Bernadette's back.

"How are you doing?" Senpai Sarah asked.

"Wow, fine, I guess..." Bernadette said, blowing out her breath. "Oops, I mean, fine, senpai."

Sarah laughed. "The moves seem so small yet so hard?"

Bernadette nodded and smiled as she wiped sweat from her brow with her towel and gulped water.

"Many of the karate moves seem minor, but they require balance and form, therefore bringing many muscle groups into play. You'll learn to develop these muscles over time, and the moves will become easier."

The next part of the class involved breathing. "You lose your power if you don't breathe properly," Sarah directed. She had them breathe in through their nose and out through their mouths with their tongues pressed on the roof of their mouths.

Bernadette saw the sense in this. Her last two sessions with Susie had left her breathless. She'd need more than just her fists to defend herself against that girl.

The class seemed to go on forever. Sensei commanded them to stop and line up. They needed to bow out. They bowed deeply to sensei and then sat on the floor for meditation.

When the class was over, Bernadette had a sense of exhilaration. What she'd learned in karate and seen in other students doing drills brought her a new understanding of martial arts.

Sensei approached her as she headed for the change room.

"May I have a moment with you?" he asked.

"Was I okay, sensei?" Bernadette asked. "I didn't mean to hold up your class. I promise I'll be much better next time—"

Sensei put up his hand and smiled. "No, Bernadette, you were fine. For someone with a leg injury you're doing as well or even better than some of my introductory white belts. I just wanted to talk to you about how you got your injury."

Sensei dropped his voice lower, to an almost conspiratorial whisper. "They bullied me in school, as well. You think a name like Krapinski didn't get me a lot of beatings?" He looked around to see if the other students were listening. "I was a little Polish Jew off the boat from Krakow. I hardly spoke English when we arrived here. And the name Krapinski, *oy vey*, the kids beat the crap out of little Krapinski whenever they had the chance."

"So then, you learned karate and beat them all up?" Bernadette asked.

Sensei shook his head and smiled. "First, I learned the proper stances of karate, and I scared them into thinking I would beat them all up."

"You bluffed, sensei?"

"Yes, I did. I don't recommend it. Someone can call your bluff," sensei said. He smiled at the memory.

He put his hand on Bernadette's shoulder. "You need to practice so it becomes second nature to you. Show yourself as confident—

then you can defend yourself. And remember, there is no first strike in karate."

Bernadette bowed deeply again, "Thank you, sensei." She walked to the change room, got out of her soaking wet gi, toweled off, and put on her street clothes.

She felt good about her first lesson. There was a lot to learn, but she was getting it quickly. Now, with practice, she would pick up the *katas* and move on to more defensive moves.

The girls were waiting anxiously for her. They were brimming with excitement for what they'd just seen. "When can we take karate lessons?" Abigail asked.

"I don't know." She turned to sensei. "Can they start karate if they want? Is there any age restriction?"

"We've started them as young as four years old. If they want, I'll set up an introductory class for them when you come," sensei said.

"Yeah," Amber said. "Karate chop, karate chop!"

Bernadette realized she'd have to pass this by her aunt, but she didn't see a problem. This would make it easier to get the kids to the sessions. "Okay, kids, next week, you're both in karate."

The kids jumped up and down with excitement. Bernadette realized all she needed to do was win more money at poker, convince her aunt this was a good idea, and find time to learn these new moves while allowing her leg to heal.

14

THE NEXT MONTH went by in a blur. Bernadette trained in karate with her little cousins. They loved the moves and the exercise. For Bernadette, martial arts gave her mind focus.

She learned how to find balance and how the arms and legs worked in punches and kicks. There were no excess movement. When her left arm blocked, her right arm remained tight by her side in the "chamber."

It sounded like loading a rifle with a bullet. When the arm came out of the chamber for a strike, the fist corkscrewed and snapped at the target. When she used a punching bag, the effect felt exhilarating. Her arms and fists became weapons. She loved to spar with the other students. Each session taught her more and pushed her harder.

She excelled in her school work and her poker games. Her winnings paid for both her cousins and her karate classes and for groceries to help her aunt.

Aunt Mary came home one day, looked around their grungy apartment, and said to Bernadette, "You know, I think it's time we move to something better, with more space."

"How about with a quieter neighborhood, less street noise and newer," Bernadette said. "There's a place on my way to school that looked nice, it's on a side street. It had a two bedroom for rent. You want me to check it out?"

Her aunt agreed, and Bernadette set out to find them a new apartment. She did not know she'd run into a stumbling block in trying to rent the place.

The apartment building did look nice, sitting two blocks off the main road, beside a small park. It had a balcony and a play area in the back.

Bernadette rang the buzzer of the Goodhue's, listed as the superintendents of the building.

A cheery ladies voice answered and she'd be right down.

"You must excuse my appearance, I'm Betty Goodhue." She said opening the door. She brushed some flour from her blouse. "I've been baking cookies all morning for our church."

She was a tall round lady in her late fifties with an easy smile, bouncy locks of blonde hair and bright blue eyes.

Bernadette smiled at her as they walked along the new hallways with fresh paint, spotless clean carpets, and sparkling light fixtures. A chandelier in the foyer bounced light off the walls, with shiny brass mailboxes that no one could tamper with because the front door had a security lock. Residents had a special keypad for entry.

Betty Goodhue smelled of vanilla and cinnamon. Bernadette breathed in her aroma and the ultra clean apartment. Betty showed her a spacious suite, with new appliances and freshly cleaned rugs. The bedrooms were large with an enormous bathroom, and, to her surprise, a second half bath with a toilet and sink. Bernadette thought they had answered the prayers of four girls.

"I'm sorry, I've been rattling away my dear. I haven't asked you who would rent this?" Betty asked when she took a breath from mentioning all the features of the place.

"It's for my aunt and her two girls, they're seven and nine, and for me." Bernadette explained. "My aunt's a server, well kind of a barmaid—but she's kind of in transition."

"Um...well that's nice...." Betty said, her voice dropping an octave.

"Well, we need more space. I'll be going to university next year, and my aunt is starting courses to be a dental hygienist." Bernadette continued.

"How wonderful," Betty said. Her eyebrows went up and her large curls bounced a bit.

Bernadette knew she had an opening. She needed to bridge the gap. "We're hoping to get an apartment in this area, as it's close to our church. We don't have a car, and as you know, winters can be harsh when standing waiting for the bus on Sundays."

Betty's eyes took on a new light. "You're church people?"

"Yes, ma'am, we attend St. John the Evangelist," Bernadette said. This wasn't too big a lie. Her aunt had said she'd been there occasionally, and Bernadette intended to go there as soon as her sins had piled up enough that she'd need confession. At this rate, it would be soon.

"That's wonderful," Betty said, with her smile back at full beam. "My husband, his name is Albert, you'll meet him later, and me, we're Lutherans. Now, we have no problem with Catholics, like them fine; there are many roads to Jesus."

Bernadette smiled and nodded her head. "Yes, there certainly are many ways to our Lord."

"Why don't you bring your aunt and cousins tomorrow. My husband will be here. He makes all the final decisions, but don't worry, you're a lovely young lady, and good Christian folks are often hard to find."

"Why thank you, ma'am—"

"Now, you just call me Betty. You're so polite and nice and such a respectful girl for your age, I wish there were more like you."

"Why thank you—Betty," Bernadette said with a shy grin.

Betty gave her a warm handshake and touched her arm as she left. Bernadette felt exhilarated as she crunched through the snow on her return to the rundown apartment. It seemed even worse now after seeing the place. She told her aunt about the place. The rent was three hundred dollars more a month than they paid at present, but with her aunt's tips and Bernadette's poker winnings, they could manage it.

The next day Aunt Mary dressed the kids in their best clothes, put on a nice pantsuit with a new winter jacket, and they headed over to the apartment. Fresh snow lay on the ground with clear blue skies and a light wind.

Bernadette had to explain a few things to her aunt Mary as they walked. She filled her in as they crunched through the snow.

"I'm studying to be a what?" Aunt Mary asked with dismay in her voice.

"A dental hygienist."

"Why not a brain surgeon?"

"I thought that'd be a bit of a stretch."

"A dental hygienist isn't? You couldn't have said a manicurist or hair stylist. Neither of those came to you?"

"I've always seen you as much smarter, Aunt Mary."

Aunt Mary laughed. "And you have us attending church every Sunday as well?" She looked down at the girls walking in front of them. "You know, there's at least one thing we can do."

"What's that?" Bernadette asked.

"Go to church on Sunday," Aunt Mary said with a wink.

They came up to the apartment, and Betty buzzed them inside. This time she wore an apron with mustard stains. "Oh, you must excuse me, I'm making sandwiches for the homeless shelter. Our church always takes over once a month," she said as she fussed over Abigail and Amber. "What pretty girls you are. I'll get you some cookies when we've finished the paperwork for the rental."

"Thank you," the girls said in unison.

"Ah, here's Albert; he's been cleaning the boiler room all morning. Sorry, he looks a mess," Betty said as Albert approached.

Albert was thin and wiry in his fifties, with thick glasses and thick arms. He wore blue jeans and a grease-stained t-shirt. A well-worn baseball cap rose high on his head, as if to give him more height. It didn't help him much, he rose to just shy of five foot six with the hat.

"Hey, Albert, wipe your hands and come meet these fine people I told you about," Betty said. She had her arms around the two girls as if she'd decided they'd be her personal charges.

Bernadette noticed Albert's face cloud over as he approached. His eyes glanced back and forth from Aunt Mary to Abigail and Amber. His gait became stilted as he walked. He slowed and stopped two metres away. He did not offer his hand in greeting.

"I rented the place," Albert said. He looked down at the carpet, as if he'd just spied some offensive stain. "I forgot to tell you, Betty. A couple came by this morning and said they'd rent it."

"But, I didn't see no couple—"

"It's gone. Sorry," Albert said. He turned on his heels and walked back up the stairs. His short legs pumping as he escaped from them as fast as he could.

"I'm so sorry..." Betty said. A Look of confusion and sadness came over her.

Bernadette looked from Betty to Albert. Something was wrong. Had Albert acted out of character? Perhaps he'd never rented to native Indians?

"We have no luck," Aunt Mary said as they walked back to their own grungy digs. Bernadette looked over her shoulder as they walked away. Albert and Betty stood in a heated discussion. She understood. The sign wasn't down. She didn't want to say anything to her Aunt Mary. An idea came to her. She had a plan.

She begged off church with Aunt Mary and the girls the following Sunday. Aunt Mary decided the idea of going to church regularly was a good one. She thought it might also change their luck. The girls had to put on their Sunday best, no tracksuits, no torn cloths. No, not for Aunt Mary. "The Lord sees what you're wearing in there," she said.

Bernadette walked to the apartment building they'd wanted to rent. The For Rent sign still hung on the front door.. She took a place behind a tree in the park and waited.

Albert and his wife left their apartment building at 9:30 am. Albert wore black dress pants, shirt and tie with a heavy leather jacket. Betty wore a faux fur coat with those silly fake sealskin boots they made fun of on the reservation.

Bernadette followed behind. Making sure she wasn't seen. As they entered the church, she took her place in the back row. The place was

Lutheran, similar to Catholic, or so she'd been told, without the pope and the Latin. Not a bad thing, she thought.

The Lutheran pastor gave a nice sermon, with the usual goodness to all men and avoiding sin. Bernadette wondered if they all didn't read the same playbook. Bernadette fell in line to leave the church after the sermon. She inched her way toward the pastor, and with smiles and nods cut her way in just in front of Albert and his wife.

The pastor brightened when he noticed Bernadette. "Ah, a new and young face to our church. Have you just moved to our city?" He was an older man with a shock of gray hair the same color as his full gray beard. At Christmas, he doubled as Santa Claus.

"Yes, I have, pastor, I've moved here from a First Nations reservation near Fort Vermilion... do you welcome First Nations people to your congregation?" Bernadette asked with a coy smile and downcast eyes.

"My child, of course we do. Lutheran churches were one of the first to welcome Canada's native people," the pastor said. He took Bernadette's hand firmly in his, pressing it as if he'd made it his goal to undo all the wrongs done to the native people.

"Thank you, pastor. How nice. I'll tell my aunt. She'll be so pleased. Now, perhaps if you can help us with one more thing."

"Of course, my child. What is it?" the pastor asked. Now he was beaming brightly, as if he'd just become God's conduit from heaven.

"We're having a hard time finding a larger apartment in this neighborhood... perhaps, if you know anyone who might assist us?"

"Why, my dear, right here is Albert and Betty Goodhue. They manage an apartment very near here. Don't you have something for this young lady and her aunt, Albert?" the pastor asked.

Albert's face turned pale. He gulped several times to catch his breath, "Well... I... I'm not sure..."

Betty pushed in front of Albert. "Why yes, we do young lady. Someone told us just today they didn't want the two-bedroom suite we have. Why not come over for tea later this afternoon, and you and your aunt can have a look?"

Bernadette shook Betty's hand. "Thank you so much, and thank you, pastor. You've been so wonderful and welcoming."

Bernadette smiled as she said goodbye to the pastor and the Goodhues. She looked forward to telling her aunt they'd be moving, and they might have to show up at a Lutheran Church once in a while.

15

SUSIE GRABBED the pack of matches off the table. She lit a cigarette and expelled a stream of blue smoke into the air. She looked at the kitchen where Stavros, the pizza restaurant owner, stared at her. He looked away quickly.

She wanted to give him the finger. She hated this place. They'd been barred from other places for fowl language, loitering, or not spending enough money for the time they spent hanging out.

Stavros was different. Susie had him figured out. When she walked to the ladies' room, she gave him a look, as if she wanted him to follow her. He never did. She figured him for a fantasy man. All imagination and no balls to get anything done, just like Leo and David who sat across from her.

Leo was the lone black kid she could recruit to her gang. He was a plus in a far north city like Canada, where there weren't many blacks. She wanted a bunch of black kids in her gang, so she could live out her fantasy of being this gangland queen of the north. It played well in her head.

Once she turned legal age—it was eighteen or nineteen—she'd get a name change. Something cool like Shabina; someone told her it was Arabic for *eye of the storm*. She'd needed a piece though, a shiny handgun. You couldn't buy one in Canada, *because it was strict and uptight, Canada is such a bore,* she thought.

Susie had wanted to lead a gang ever since she'd returned from Los Angeles with her parents. They'd gone to Disney Land. The vacation had been wonderful, a dream for an impressionable ten-year-old steeped in fantasy. Her parents used the trip to tell her they were getting a divorce.

She trusted no one after that. Her attitude and grades dropped. Her change to a bad ass suited her just fine. She blew another stream of smoke and smiled at Stavros at the pizza window. She winked at him. He ducked back inside his kitchen.

"What we going to do about the bitch, Bernadette?" Leo asked. He was doodling on the back of a napkin. One dreadlock hung down his face. Susie told him he looked cool with dreadlocks. It made his hat sit funny on his head, and he didn't like it, but Susie wasn't to be ignored.

Susie's eyes snapped back to focus on him. "What about her? I can finish her any time I want."

David shook his head, "Nah, Susie, you mess with her, you get in a shit load a trouble. The cops be looking to put you in juvie. Hey girl, right now, here you are smoking a cigarette, and the law changed this year to eighteen to smoke. Those shit head cops can put you in juvie for jus' that. You get what I mean?"

Susie reached forward and grabbed David's hand; she dug her fingernails hard until he yelped. "Don't you ever tell me what I can do, you useless tit."

David nursed his hand. "Jesus, Susie... I'm trying to help."

"He's sweet on you, Susie," Leo said. He gave a little snort at this own joke and took a big gulp of his Pepsi.

"You're both dumb tits. I just don't know which is the dumbest," Susie said. She pounded her cigarette into the ashtray. "Hey, Stavros, how about another coke?"

Stavros poked his head out, "Sure, how bout you order a pizza or something. You think I feed my family with you drinking three cokes all afternoon?"

"You don't want me to get too fat now, do you, Stavros?" Susie asked in coy tone. She turned towards him, drawing attention to her growing bosoms.

Stavros waved his hand in the air and disappeared back in the kitchen.

"I heard Bernadette be going to some kind of karate class the past month," Leo said.

"Ain't going to help her," Susie said. "I'll kick her ass all the same."

"But you can't get close to her," David said quietly, pulling both his hands under the table in case Susie wanted to claw him again.

"You're a double dumb tit, David. But you got a point. None of us can take on the wrestling team. Those jocks are bad ass," Susie said.

"So, what're you going to do? We just let little karate girl pal around with her chaperons and smile at us like we can't get to her?" Leo asked.

Susie lit another cigarette and flashed her eyes as Stavros delivered her a coke. "I got some things up my sleeve. I have a way to get to her—I'll kick her little ass yet."

She blew anther stream of smoke into the air, and and smiled. She hadn't felt this good in a long time.

16

BERNADETTE HATED PEOPLE WHO SAID, "*Never get too optimistic, because something bad will come your way.*" It happened one week after finding the new apartment.

The following week, after the visit to the new apartment, all Bernadette and her aunt and the kids could talk about was how they'd furnish the new place. They'd made a trip by bus to the big Ikea store, and with the extensive catalogue of strange-sounding Swedish names for odd-looking furniture in hand, they collectively plotted their new home.

There would be bunk beds for the kids, a loft bed with a desk underneath for Bernadette, and simple fabric sofa and two armchairs for the living room. They'd given notice on their present place and crossed the days off on the calendar until they moved.

Then something changed in Aunt Mary. She was going to work at the tavern later than usual. They'd meet coming in the door. Bernadette sensed something in her aunt's face—it was fear.

When Bernadette had touched her arm, Aunt Mary pulled it away with a pained look on her face. "You want to tell me what's going on with you?" she asked.

"It's nothing," Aunt Mary said, but her eyes said volumes.

Bernadette sent the kids to the bedroom to play. "Your nothing, seems to have some pain attached. You're not good at hiding things—we have that in common."

Aunt Mary broke down in tears. "It was the big guy—the one you threw out of the apartment. He goes by the name of Ace, but his name is Guy... something."

"He's hassling you at the tavern?"

"Yeah, he's been grabbing me when I go by his table... and... last night he tried to force me into the men's room with him. I was lucky, our cook was walking by and told him to leave me alone," Aunt Mary said.

"Why doesn't the manager throw him out?" Bernadette asked.

"The manager is chicken shit. This guy belongs to a bike gang, and he's afraid he'll bring the other bikers in and tear up the place. He told me I was the problem. I could either take it or quit."

"Wow, that is chickenshit."

"Hey, watch your language, young lady."

They laughed, hugged hard, and Aunt Mary left for work. The next morning when she returned home, Bernadette got up to check on her. She seemed fine. The rough guy named Ace hadn't shown up, and she'd had a good shift and made lots of tips.

Bernadette hoped they could deal with it. Maybe Ace had got his rocks off annoying her aunt and would move on. Then she received a note from her homeroom teacher. She was to call Officer Myers at the local police station as soon as possible.

She waited until after her last morning class to phone Officer Myers. The pay phones near the gym were the least used and the least conspicuous. She dialed the number and got Myers on her cell phone.

"What's up?" Bernadette asked.

"I need to see you; there's been a development."

"What kind of development?" Bernadette asked. She watched three girls walking down the corridor. They were talking loudly and singing the new tune "*Crying*" by Aerosmith. Bernadette covered her one ear to block out the noise. "I said, what kind of development?"

"Can you get over here?" Myers asked.

Bernadette sighed loudly. "Sure, I'll be there right away."

Her problem was no escort. Travis and the team were in the gym doing drills for an upcoming wrestling match. She didn't want to bother them. Dumping her books in her locker, she headed out from the school on her own.

She made it to the local police station with no problem. There wasn't one of Susie's gang around. The day was getting warm. The snow was melting from a mild breeze, and big, fluffy clouds blew across a bright blue sky.

A front desk receptionist took Bernadette to a back office where Officer Myers was waiting.

"Hey, Bernadette, thanks for coming in so soon. I understand you've been doing great in class the past month. Sensei feels you're a natural. He's impressed by your attitude and determination... can I offer you a soft drink, water, or tea?" Myers said.

"I'm fine. Glad I impressed sensei, I was afraid he'd throw me out the first session."

Myers laughed. "He ejects those who talk in class or don't try hard enough. You're good."

Bernadette looked down at the desk, then up at Myers. "I'm sorry, but I don't have a lot of time, I need to get back to my next class. What's this about?"

Myer's arched an eyebrow at Bernadette's forthright question. "You're right, and I need to get to the point." She pulled out a file folder from the side of her desk. "Our detachment got this fax from the RCMP detachment near your reservation. Do you remember a Sergeant McNeil?"

"Of course I do," Bernadette said. "He suggested I leave the reservation after... well, after a minor incident."

"The incident blew up. In this memo, the sergeant says, and I paraphrase, the town's kids discovered the lie told by the Cardinal boys and wanted to beat the hell out of them." Myers sat back in her chair. "Basically, Bernadette, the three Cardinal boys mentioned here have left the reservation and are looking for you."

Bernadette shrugged. "So? They can search all they want, they don't know I have an aunt here."

"Well, now they do."

"How'd they find out?"

"When your aunt Mary phoned your grandmother, your grand-mother's phone wasn't working, so she called the general store to get hold of her. A guy named... Gus, he went to get your grandmother to get her to the phone."

"Oh my god, not Gus," Bernadette said as she put her hand over her forehead and sighed. "He's the biggest gossip on the reservation." She put her hands down on the desk. "So the Cardinal boys know I'm in Edmonton. Big city, lots of high schools. By the time they find me, I'll be heading for university."

"Sure, if it weren't for this news article," Myers said. She pulled a paper and shoved it across the desk.

It was from the local town's paper. The article read about Bernadette Callahan, the upcoming track star savagely beaten in the shower at Western High in Edmonton.

"How did this get out?" Bernadette asked.

"Simple," Myers said. "they called the police to the high school. All the newspaper reporters have police scanners, and someone at the hospital or your school must have blabbed, and your little northern town newspaper picked it up last week."

"Damn it. I'm screwed."

"Yeah, pretty much," Myers said. "Do you have any family you can go to in another province? Maybe even somewhere in the United States?"

"You want me to run?"

"I called Sergeant McNeil, to see the trouble you might be in with the Cardinal boys, and he thinks this is serious. You made them lose face up there. You kicked their ass—they lied about it and got found out. He said they were muttering about killing you."

"Wait a minute, isn't threatening to kill someone against the law?" Bernadette asked. She sat upright in her chair, staring hard at Myers.

Officer Myers nodded. "Yes, it is, but in this case it's just hearsay.

What Constable McNeil heard was from another source. We'd have to get the witness to say they'd heard the Cardinals say it and have them make a statement."

Bernadette sank back in her chair. "The Cardinal boys have threatened most people on the reservation for the slightest thing. Doubt if anyone would come forward for me."

"So, you'll find somewhere to go?"

Bernadette shook her head. "I need to take care of my aunt Mary. I don't like the situation she's in."

"Something I can help with?"

Bernadette pursed her lips and paused for a moment. Should she confide in Myers? It took her a second to decide. "Some guy by the nickname Ace has been hassling my aunt at the tavern. His name is Guy, something—."

"Guy Labinski," Myers said. "He's a badass. We've been trying to arrest him for months on drug trafficking. He's the one supplying drugs to your school."

"My school? I had no idea."

Myers looked at Bernadette. "Bernadette, Ace is dangerous. He's been dealing drugs to a gang at your school."

"Susie's gang?"

"You got it."

"Why haven't you been able to arrest Ace? Wait—you can't catch him in the act. That's it, isn't it?" Bernadette asked, her words came out fast, as if she'd just discovered the answer to a math problem.

"My, you're a quick study. We have no one to infiltrate the gang, and no one school age to approach Ace for a buy," Myers intoned. She wondered if what she was doing was right. The detachment had considered approaching a student so many times but held off— the implications of bringing a child into a drug bust was reprehensible... but Bernadette seemed different, she was older than her years.

"What if I helped you nab Ace?" Bernadette asked.

"Bernadette, this isn't some game. We're talking about an undercover operation. You'd be wearing a wire, and I'd need to get the

Crown Prosecutor involved to allow you to do it. Otherwise, the whole thing gets thrown out of court if we don't do it right."

"How long's it going to take?"

Myers rubbed her hands together. "Can you give me a minute? The officers in the narcotics squad are here right now." She disappeared for a moment and came back with a man and a woman in tow.

"This is Detectives Mark Salenko and Denise Kruger; they do undercover work in narcotics. Detectives, this is Bernadette Callahan. She's offered to work undercover and do a drug buy from Ace and his gang."

Bernadette looked them over. Mark wore a white muscle shirt tucked into blue jeans. Tattoos covered his arms. He'd tied his long black hair into a ponytail. He looked more hard-core trucker than a detective.

Denise Kruger wore a tight leather skirt and her face was covered in makeup and bad eyeliner. A tight leopard skin blouse was low cut, showing off her ample cleavage.

"Your detectives?" Bernadette asked with a big dose of wonder in her voice.

Kruger snapped her chewing gum. "Yeah, aren't we a sight? But dressing like this gets us in tight with the locals." She turned to Myers. "What's it you want us to do with this kid?"

"I'd go undercover. I could wear a wire and do a drug buy. Put Ace in the slammer," Bernadette said. She sat forward in her chair. This all made perfect sense to her.

"How old are you?" Salenko asked.

"Sixteen—but I'll be seventeen soon." Bernadette said.

"Holy shit, Myers, you're not serious? We can't work with kids," Salenko said.

"But, what about *21 Jump Street*? They had all these detectives who acted like high school students to do drug busts and stuff. I'd just be doing it as a real high school student. This would be a natural for me," Bernadette said.

"Yeah, a natural pain in the ass," Salenko said. He looked over at

Myers. "You'll never get this past the Crown Prosecutor. Matter of fact, if you even bring it downtown, you're making a major C.L.M."

"What's a C.L.M?" Bernadette asked.

"It's a career-limiting move," Kruger said. "Police officers only get so many in their job. Making a request like this would have the legal suits downtown put a note on Officer Myer's file. Not good, Myers, seriously not good."

"And don't involve us in this, Myers, 'cause we'd never go along on this." Salenko said. He turned to Bernadette. "No offense, kid, but I got a wife and two kids and a mortgage to pay. I may act the part of a scumbag drug dealer, but I've had fifteen years in the force. They may use kids down in the US in this *21 Jump Street* thing—"

"It's a TV show," Kruger said.

"Okay, better yet, it's not real. In actual life, we don't use anyone under eighteen in our activities. We're close to cracking Ace on our own. He's part of the Devils Undertakers biker gang." Salenko looked at Myers and smiled. "The leader of the gang, he doesn't take to dealing drugs to schools."

Kruger laughed. "Yeah, get this, he's a really family type. Got kids in hockey. Sells his meth to university and colleges. A man with a conscience."

"All we gotta do," Salenko said, "is get the goods on Ace, let his gang leader find out he's dealing to high schools, and he's done. They'll take him out for us." He turned to leave. "So thanks for the offer, but you best get back to school and quit watching silly American television. We do genuine work here in Canada."

They walked out of the room. Myers and Bernadette sat there in silence. They had shot their idea down. Myers sniffed, pulled out a tissue from a box on her desk, and blew her nose softly. "I guess that's it then. You need to find a new place to live."

Bernadette's fingers dug into the sides of her chair. "No, that's not it. I'm not going anywhere." Her eyes narrowed. "One of the first things I learned in karate is *sanchin*—the three battles—"

Myers nodded. "Yes, the three battles of the mind and body, sight and perception and breath, there are many distinct elements of each—"

Bernadette put up her hand. "Sorry, I don't need a refresher lesson. What I'm saying is, I have three battles of Susie, Ace, and the Cardinals. I'm not sure how I'll handle it, but running away isn't one of them."

Myers shook her head. "I can't make you do anything. I can advise you, you're putting your life in danger by staying where you are."

Bernadette got up from the chair. "Thanks, officer, consider me advised. Now, I've classes to attend."

Bernadette left the police station, crossed the street, and walked towards the school. The complexity of the situation was rolling around in her head when she turned a corner and stopped. Two of Susie's gang stood at the end of the street.

17

BERNADETTE STOOD at the corner watching the two boys. Had they seen her? Were they about to move away? They stood midway up the block, puffing on cigarettes and staring at the road. They were waiting for something.

A car drove slowly by and stopped in front of them. Bernadette crossed the street, making like she was heading somewhere else. She found a large mailbox to hide behind to observe the boys.

No one got out of the car—a hand reached out with a package. The larger boy, Bernadette remembered as Leo, took the package and jammed it into his jacket. He looked up and down the street. He didn't notice Bernadette.

The car drove away. She memorized the car and the license number. How could these boys associate with someone who drove a late model Cadillac?

Checking her wristwatch, she realized she needed to get to class. These boys were no longer anything but a hindrance to her and an essential math test. This was mid terms, and she needed to get this test done or lose whatever marks she already had.

She moved out from behind the mailbox and walked down the

street. She made it a few hundred metres when a boy yelled, "Hey, it's the Karate Kid."

She continued walking, head down, concentrating on walking on the icy sidewalk.. If she was lucky, whatever they received from the car was more important than her.

"Hey, I'm talking to you," one boy said. Their footsteps sounded as they crossed the street. They stood in front of her. Leo stood tall, his lower lip showing attitude, dominance. He crossed his arms to show he wasn't about to let her pass.

Bernadette stopped, eyeing Leo and the other boy. "I need to get to class; please get out of my way."

"Ha, you can't take on Susie, how you gonna take on both of us, you little shit?"

Bernadette eyed both the boys. There was no talking to them, and no way she'd outrun them.

She rooted herself, making her stance square with her palms raised. Her eyes flicked over Leo as he approached.

"Oh, my, I'm so scared," Leo said. He looked at his sidekick. "She got some kind of Kung Foo, or Hai Karate moves, don't she, David?"

David smiled and nodded. "Maybe she'll show you some?"

Bernadette focused on David for a second. His pupils large. She looked back at Leo. His were the same—she'd seen it on the Cardinal boys. They were both stoned.

Her best guess was marijuana. It would make them slower. She was going to find out.

"I ain't scared a no Kung Fu horse shit," Leo said, walking towards her, his right hand balled into a fist.

She waited for Leo to get into her striking range. She deflected his fist with a left arm block. His swing brought him in close. Her hand had already gone into a chambered position. It came out like a tight corkscrew rocket connecting with his nose.

"Jesusmotherfuckingchrist!" Leo yelled as he hit the ground.

"Wow, you like, broke his nose," David said.

"You want to be next?" Bernadette asked. She resumed her stance. She was ready for anything David threw at her.

"No, no, no," David said.

"Grab your friend and get the hell out of here. I got classes to get to, and you're a pain in the ass," Bernadette said.

David grabbed Leo's arm to pull him up and move him out of Bernadette's path. A stream of blood from Leo's nose made bright patterns on the snow.

Bernadette walked past them. Her knees were trembling; she walked as fast as possible, favoring her right leg with an attempt to hide her limp. *Never show a predator you have an injury,* she told herself. David might try to attack her in his stoned state.

She got to class before the test started. It took her a few minutes to focus. Math wasn't her easiest subject, but with the help of Melinda in the past month she could get the gist of variables and exponents in algebra.

The clock on the wall seemed to race by as she struggled to make her mind focus on math problems over the fight she'd had in the street. Would Leo and David come after her later? Sure they would. Would Susie take offense to this—what was she thinking? She'd just declared war on their gang by beating up Leo.

A simple punch in the nose was all it took to drop Leo. A knee in the groin had dropped Tommy. Her simple one-act strikes were getting her into deep trouble.

The teacher called, "Time's up," and the class turned their test papers over. Bernadette hoped she focused enough to give the right answers.

Even if she had to make a run for it to avoid the Cardinals, she didn't want to leave with bad test scores, as eventually she needed to get back to her schooling. She filed out of class and found Travis waiting for her.

"Hey, Travis," Bernadette said, not trying to sound head over heels infatuated with him.

"Hey, Bernadette," Travis said, taking her by the arm and leading her to the side of the hallway. "Someone said you punched Leo in the nose. Is it true, or has somebody been smoking something?"

Bernadette hated the expression of disappointment on Travis's face. She'd promised him she wouldn't get into any fights and always wait for him to escort her anytime she left school.

She shrugged and looked down at the floor. "Yeah, it's not a rumor. I met officer Myers today... on my own... sorry, and Leo and David tried to stop me from getting back to class."

"You promised me, Bernadette, you said I'd be the one to watch after you..."

Bernadette looked up at Travis. He wasn't mad; there was a tear in his eye. He was concerned for her. "Oh, my god, Travis, I'm sorry... I..."

"It's okay," Travis said. He rubbed her shoulder, and somehow she fell into a hug from him. It felt wonderful.

She looked up at him and kissed him on the cheek. "I will always be sure to enlist my valiant knight, Sir Travis, before I sally forth to do battle with the dragons outside these walls."

"You'd better," Travis said. "We Knights work hard for our wages."

"Wages? What payment are you expecting, fair knight?"

Travis bent down and planted a warm kiss on her lips. "Just this, fair maiden."

Bernadette's knees almost buckled. Her first kiss from a boy— well, a real boy, and not some little kid planting a pretend smooch on her in fifth grade.

"Ah, handsome knight, it is a fair bargain for your services," Bernadette said when she finally caught her breath. She was about to get him to repeat the kiss when she noticed something.

It was a face that startled her. For a moment she thought she recognized Peter Cardinal. She pulled back from Travis and stared down the hall.

"Did you see a ghost? Are you all right?" Travis asked.

"I thought I recognized somebody from my village up north," Bernadette said.

"A good somebody or a not-so-good somebody?" Travis asked, staring into her eyes.

How could she lie to him about the Cardinal boys? He wanted to protect her, and he needed to know about them. "I think I need to fill you in on a few things," she said.

18

PETER CARDINAL GOT into the back seat of the 1973 two-door Chevy Malibu. Tommy and Stephen sat in the front. Peter felt sick about the car. The car belonged to Gus, the old man he worked for. He'd helped them steal it.

Tommy said it wasn't stealing as the keys were in the ignition, and besides, Gus drove it in the summer. He wouldn't miss it until spring.

But Peter knew Gus would notice a barren spot in the snow where the car had been. Gus would figure out Peter had taken it. Peter's heart had sunk the moment they'd got in it and left for the city.

Peter did the books for Gus's store. His work made him proud, gave him satisfaction. He added up the figures at the store and did inventory once a month, but Peter secretly loved it. He'd fallen in love with numbers. They gave him a sense of accomplishment. It removed him from his cousins—he became his own person at Gus's place. Like he mattered.

Tommy and Stephen pulled him along. He did whatever they said, as if he had no will of his own.

He didn't want to be here. He wanted to finish high school, take the required college courses to become a certified general accountant, and then work for a large oil company in the city. Maybe he'd even get transferred overseas. In Dubai or Saudi, he'd be just another brown person. He could disappear.

He sensed he was disappearing now. He stared out the window, his breath fogged the glass and blocked his view.

"Was she there?" Tommy asked.

"Yeah, she's with some huge white dude," Stephen said.

"Did she see you guys?"

"Nah, not a chance. We were careful, weren't we Peter?"

Peter looked up from his fogged window; he barely understood the question. "Yeah, we stayed out of sight."

"Good, 'cause we warriors are on the prowl, we gonna kick that little half-breed's ass. When they find out she's disappeared, nobody will fuck with the Cardinal boys. Ain't that right," Tommy said.

"Damn right," Stephen said.

Peter looked out the window. His sigh completely fogged the back window.

19

After Bernadette came clean with Travis about the Cardinal boys, he was even more vigilant. He made sure he or one of his wrestling team walked with her to pick up her cousins and safely to her apartment.

When she had karate practice, there was a bodyguard; when she took the kids to the pool or to shop for groceries, there was a shadow with her.

Susie and her gang kept their distance. There wasn't another Cardinal boys sighting, and Bernadette was spending a lot more time with Travis. She was, in his words, "Paying him handsomely with kisses," which were making her young heart almost "fluffy," as if she could find a word for it.

This wasn't solving her problem with Ace. She needed a plan to take out Ace and to keep herself out of the reaches of the Cardinals.

The more she wracked her brain, the more she understood she needed to bring in some much needed help. Her best choice was Melinda. She wasn't good in a fight; it was because Melinda was a brain, an honest-to-goodness genius. An honors student who had already decided she'd go into pre-med and pursue a career as a cardiothoracic surgeon. Bernadette had to research the designation.

It was heart, lungs, and all the good stuff that made the human body function in the chest cavity.

Bernadette caught up with Melinda in study hall. "Hey, Melinda," she said as she plunked her books down beside her.

Melinda brushed a wisp of her fine blonde hair from her perfectly blue eyes. "Hey, Bernadette, I hear you're kicking it with karate classes. Pretty soon, you'll be able to protect the wrestling team."

Bernadette smiled. Melinda's humor was bone dry, but it was good. "Yeah, I'm the new karate queen." She leaned forward across the table and lowered her voice. "Listen, Melinda, I got this sticky situation. I need to kind of record someone without them knowing about it. Any idea how I'd go about it?"

Melinda looked up at Bernadette, pushing her glasses to the bridge of her nose. "Are we talking entrapment here?"

"Whoa, you're lightening fast, girl."

Melinda shifted in her chair and adjusted her glasses. "Be straight with me, Bernadette, I'll help with you with anything, but I need to understand what your involved in."

Bernadette's shoulders sagged; she leaned forward, took Melinda's hand, and told her about Ace, his drug deals, his bothering her aunt and the Cardinal boys. When she'd finished, she'd felt like she'd gotten off a psychiatrist's couch—or imagined what it felt like if she'd been on one.

Melinda squeezed her hand. "Why didn't you tell me? My older brother, Jason, has a digital recorder he uses for his classes at university. I'll get it from him. Sounds like we got to get a persona for you this Ace will trust."

"A persona?"

"Yeah, if he thinks you're in the drug game, he'll incriminate himself. You can't go in there as you. You got to go in there and get in this guy's face—be someone who will draw his attention, some hyped-up bitch." Melinda put her hands over her mouth. "I can't believe I said that."

"You're onto to something, Melinda. I need to draw out the black wolf in Ace."

"You've lost me. What's the black wolf?"

"It's the angry one. I get his attention and get him mad, he'll say things to incriminate himself. I record it, give it to the police, and he's done," Bernadette said.

Melinda shook her head. "I'm not sure if that works."

"Why not? We got his voice on a recording. If I get him to admit he's selling drugs at our school and using Susie as his network—why can't the police use it?"

Melinda chewed on her pen. "My brother's best friend is a second year law student at the university. I'll call him and find out if we're going in the right direction."

She took a piece of lined paper from her binder and took notes. "Okay, we check on the legality of the recording, then we find a place to do it." She tapped her pen on her chin. "Right, we need surveillance."

"Surveillance?"

Melinda pointed her pen at Bernadette. "Yes, we need to track this Ace guy and find the best place to approach him."

"Ah. He hangs out at my aunt's tavern... how about if we simply watch the place?"

"Excellent choice. I'll have my brother and his friends put a tail on the place," Melinda said.

Bernadette put a hand to her forehead. "Melinda, you put a tail on a person... never mind. Now, how are you going to get your brother's friends in on this?"

Melinda smiled. "My brother is a computer science major, all his buddies are geeks. When they're not in the computer lab, they play Mortal Kombat and Doom for hours. I tell them I've got this cool stake out, and they'll be on it with cameras and recording devices."

Bernadette rolled her eyes. "Great, we've got a geek squad up against a bike gang and drug pushers—should be good."

"Now," Melinda said, "we've got to get you a cell phone."

"A cell phone, whoa girl, those things are expensive; I can't afford one."

Melinda raised her eyebrows. "Not a problem, my father is a surgeon. He has like three cell phones. He keeps telling me he wants me to have one so I can keep in touch. Well... now's the time. While we're at it, we'll get two, and a pager so you're the image of a real drug dealer."

Bernadette shook her head. "Your dad's a doctor, and you're going to this school?"

Melinda shrugged. "My dad doesn't like the private school system. He never attended one and figured a tough school would one day make me a tough surgeon."

Bernadette looked around the room at the other students. A few looked like they'd done time in jail. "Yep, your dad knows how to practice some tough love. When do we implement this battle plan?"

"I'm going to get on the phone the moment I get home. I'll have the cell phones, plus a list of times my brother's friends will do the stakeout, you'll of course supply Ace's description, and we're ready."

"You're amazing, Melinda, I did not realize you were this good," Bernadette said as she got up from the table.

"Hey, I've seen every episode of *21 Jump Street*. I love it. It's how I relax after my studies."

Bernadette walked out of the study hall. She wondered how close their actions would mimic the television show. She remembered some people got shot in the show.

20

THREE DAYS LATER, Melinda met Bernadette in the school corridor; she lowered her voice and raised her eyebrows. "It's a go."

"What's a go?"

Melinda cast furtive glances around her. "I've got it all in place. We need to meet right after our last class. I've asked my brother and his friends to meet at my house. Can you make it?"

Bernadette had to think it over; she picked up Amber and Abigail after school, but her classes finished early and so did Melinda's. "As long as I'm out of there by three-thirty to pick up my cousins, I'm fine with it... and what do we tell Travis and the wrestling team?"

"I got it covered," Melinda said. "I checked detention hall, and Susie, our gangland queen, is in there until five." She let out a low chuckle as she said, "Apparently our little mobster got caught smoking in the girls' washroom. And Travis and his team are in a late afternoon practice. I told him we'd be in study hall together."

"Yeah, but what about her gang?"

"Are you kidding, her gang won't take you on with what you did to David and Leo—you is one bad mother—frugger," Melinda said.

Bernadette shook her head. "You don't quite have it right, but then... no, it's good. Let's go."

The walk to Melinda's place was long. She lived on the good side of town. They walked by the small bungalows and low-level apartments and crossed a big avenue into a gated community. An expensive stone fence with brass lettering announced the neighborhood's name, to make it clear that only those with money or big incomes could afford to live here. Bernadette sensed herself growing smaller as they passed the massive homes.

Melinda walked up to her house, punched in her security code, and ushered Bernadette inside. The place looked opulent to Bernadette. Hardwood floors were scattered with expensive carpets that had tables and chairs with good taste sitting on them. Fine art adorned the walls. Custom curtains on large windows let in light with an expensive glow.

Bernadette followed Melinda as they moved from room to room. She realized the home was as big as the entire fifteen-suite apartment building she lived in. She shook her head, taking it all in, realizing she'd never seen rich before. This was it.

Four young men sat in the kitchen who could have been mistaken for boys. Three wore baggy jeans and sweatshirts, with hair in different styles of disarray. One looked like he'd stepped out of *GQ Quarterly* and was merely slumming with this motley crew.

"Jason, Chad, Craig, and Aaron, this is Bernadette," Melinda said.

"Hi, Bernadette," they said in unison once they washed down the nacho chips they were stuffing in their mouths with swigs of coke.

"We hear you got a situation you want this geek posse to look after," Chad said with a smile. He was dumpy in a cute sort of way, Bernadette thought. His hair was a mess of black curls, an oversized sweatshirt covering his large body, and he hunched over the counter as if he needed to hold on to it and keep it stable.

"I really appreciate you guys getting involved in this," Bernadette said. "But I don't want you getting into trouble over my situation."

Craig snorted, coke coming out his nose. "Hell no, we exist for trouble." He wiped the coke from his nose. He was smaller than Chad, with an elfin quality that made him seem like Chad's sidekick. His friends looked at him, shaking their heads.

"Ah, what my two eloquent friends are saying is we're happy to help," Jason said. He looked very much like Melinda, the blonde hair, blue eyes, and a calm smile. "No one likes to see people bullied, and often the police can't do anything about it. We'll do whatever we can to put his Ace guy in the slammer... now, speaking of that, I brought Aaron along, our law student, to give us the inside dope on this."

Aaron sat up, wiped his glasses with a cloth from this pocket, and took out a large legal pad and pencil. He waited until his silence had the room's full attention and began in a slow monotone. "Well, as I see this case, we have the young Bernadette here, attempting to draw a confession on tape from the suspect, Ace, a.k.a Guy Labinski, is that correct?"

Bernadette shifted uncomfortably and swallowed. This felt like an interrogation. "Yes," she replied in a squeak.

Aaron made a note on his legal pad. He was better dressed than the rest; he wore gray corduroys, a blue button-down shirt, and black shiny loafers. Bernadette thought he looked all business.

"And you, Bernadette, you've had some prior dealings with this man? I understand from Melinda you threw him out of your apartment for an attempted assault of your aunt?" Aaron asked. His voice went up slightly on the last few words.

"Well, yes, but I... it wasn't really assault, he was being rough with my aunt..."

"Just answer the question."

"Yes, I threw him out of the apartment," Bernadette admitted with a sigh.

Aaron turned to his friends. "We got a problem. One, if I was the defense council for Guy Labinski, I'd say Bernadette here had a grudge against him and was seeking to entrap him for revenge, and two, and this is the most important," he looked at Bernadette, "you give a recording to the police and they put this guy in jail, he's out on bail in twenty-four hours until the hearing. The case will take months before it goes to court, and you..."

"And I'm in serious jeopardy of getting taken out by him," Bernadette said. "Is that what you're trying to say?"

"Yes, that's the extent of it," Aaron said. "I'm sorry to say this, but even with my geek squad friends on your side doing all kinds of magic with electronic listening devices, the legal system churns at a snail's pace. All the while, it puts your life in peril."

"That's not fair," Melinda said.

"It's called due process, Melinda," Aaron said. "The state must respect all legal rights owed to a person. Due process balances the power of law of the land and protects the individual from it. Ace gets the same process—even though you say he's a scumbag, he's a scumbag with rights."

"We're screwed before we get started," Chad said. He looked at his friends. "Well, geek squad, this was a good idea."

"Wait," Bernadette said. "I heard a detective say Ace was dealing drugs at the high school, he's in a gang... called the Devil's Undertakers, and his leader, a guy named... Carl Hoffer, was against it. What if we got Ace to admit what he was doing on tape and gave it to his gang leader?"

"And the gang makes Ace disappear?" Aaron said.

"Yeah, that's it," Bernadette said. "Kind of divine justice of the pack; it happens all the time in the wild, when an alpha wolf takes over, and it banishes ones that contest its leadership. And it would take away the supply of Susie's gang."

Aaron shook his head. "We're talking more than banishment here, Bernadette. I've seen some court cases on the Devil's Undertakers; they're one step away from the Hell's Angels. Their leader is a psycho named Carl Hoffer, and yes, he doesn't believe in selling drugs to schools, but he's into heavy drugs to prostitution."

"But it's the perfect solution," Chad said. "Bernadette gets Ace to admit he's selling drugs to schools on tape, we give the tape to Hoffer, and no more Ace." He picked up a nacho chip. "Problem solved." He made a loud crunch to prove his point.

"I can't be party to this," Aaron said. "I do not want to know anything more about this discussion." He looked at Jason. "You have some strange friends, and I suggest you send this little girl back under the rock from where you found her, She's nothing but trouble."

Jason stood up. "Aaron, that's rude. Bernadette is Melinda's good friend. We don't back out on our friends in my family."

Melinda stood beside Bernadette and put her arm around her. They watched Aaron pack his things into his shiny black briefcase and leave.

Chad muttered "*asshole*" in his direction as Aaron slammed the door.

The room was silent. Chad, Craig, and Jason swigged their cokes and looked at each other. Jason raised his head, looked up at the ceiling. "We can't be certain Hoffer would kill Ace?"

"No, we can't," Chad said.

"Is it our concern how this gang hands out punishment for disobedience to its credo?" Jason said.

"Hell, no," Craig said.

Jason looked at Bernadette. "We're in."

"But what about what Aaron said?" Bernadette asked.

Jason shrugged. "Look, Aaron sees incidents in black—there is no white with him. He'll make an excellent lawyer one day, but hopefully, he won't be so uptight. And don't worry about our little heated exchange. Two days from now, he'll be calling me up to go for a beer. He doesn't have any other friends."

"Okay," Melinda said. "We've got work to do."

"Right," Chad said. "I made out list of things we'll need: binoculars, cameras with telephoto lenses, the digital tape recorder, and the ten thousand dollars."

"Ten thousand dollars! Where're we going to get that kind of money?" Bernadette asked.

Chad smiled. "The University of Alberta Business Department." He pulled out a brown bill and placed it on the table. "This is the miracle of an expensive, color laser printer. All you need is some excellent paper and Voila, you got some brown one-hundred-dollar notes. We even got the new shiny metallic patch to show up, which makes it seem legit."

"Oh, my god, it's counterfeit. What are we getting ourselves into?" Bernadette said.

"If you print both sides, it's illegal." Chad turned the bill over; it was blank on the other side. "We're going to make you a big roll of these babies. As long as you have the bills rolled up, the big Ace doesn't recognize you've got bogus notes. You flash the roll like you own the Bank of Canada."

"Speaking of which," Craig said, "here's some talking points—on how drug terms. You want to be buying eight balls, that's... three and half grams. They cost 175 each. We think you'll get his attention if you ask him for ten grand worth."

"But... what if he wants to study the money... you know, like handle it," Bernadette said.

"Not going to happen," Jason said. He knitted his eyebrows into a blond frown. "You've got to be tough. You show him the roll, tell him he doesn't get any cash until you inspect the merchandise, and you're going to be distributor to all the high schools."

"But what if he wants to make a transaction right there?" Bernadette asked.

Chad scratched his head. "Good point, what does she do?"

"Ah, we have her take half the money. She flashes some cash, says there's more where this came from, and set up a buy," Craig said.

"But there won't be a buy, right?" Melinda asked.

"Nope, we get Ace saying he wants to sell drugs to Bernadette to distribute to the high schools. We drop the tape on this crazy bike leader's doorstep, and goodbye Ace."

"Sounds simple," Bernadette said. "But you know this Ace guy is pretty tough. One slip up, and somebody gets hurt. I don't want it to be any of you. You have no dog in this fight. Sorry, old Indian term... it means—"

"We know what it means, Bernadette," Jason said. "Here's how we perceive it. Your aunt's being bullied by this guy. And this guy is selling drugs at your school. So, we are in this fight. Maybe we're geek vigilantes, but here we are."

"God, I'm pumped with this, how about you guys?" Chad asked, pounding the kitchen counter.

Bernadette shook her head. "I'm just asking you to stay as far from Ace as possible. Do whatever surveillance you need to do from a distance. I can give you his description of his car, and I have his license plate number."

Jason said, "Good, we can go from there. Melinda is going to give you a cell phone to carry with you at all times. She'll have one as well, and so will we. We'll figure out a time to get you in front of him and do the recording."

"I'm so grateful to you for doing all this," Bernadette said. "You do not know how much this means to my aunt, her children, and me."

Craig put his head on Chad's shoulder. "Oh god, I'm going to tear up."

Chad pushed Craig away. "Sorry for my idiot friend, he was once a drama major, or should I say—drama queen."

Jason pulled some papers and some DVDs from his backpack. "Here are the drug definitions you must memorize, and also, we have some movies you'll want to watch."

Bernadette looked at the DVD's. "Why do I want to watch movies?"

"Get the lingo down," Chad said. "You gotta have the right attitude."

Bernadette looked at the movies. "*Goodfellas, Bad Lieutenant,* and *Debbie Does Dallas*?"

Craig looked away, his face taking on a slight red shade. "We thought a wide spectrum... to broaden your horizons in the world of crime... and such..."

Melinda shook her head. "I'm really not sure about you guys."

Jason stood up. "Do your homework, we'll gather our resources and contact you when we have a sighting of our Ace subject." He turned to Melinda. "You still got us Mom's minivan for the week."

"Yeah, but be careful with it. She just got it out of the shop from the ding she put in it," Melinda said.

"Oh, I hope it's a stealth minivan," Chad said. "'Cause we'll be way too obvious in a new Town and Country with all those windows."

"We'll cover up the windows," Jason said.

Bernadette walked to the door. She hugged Melinda on the doorstep. "This is amazing, what you're doing."

Melinda shook her head. "No, remember, you're the one who has to pull this off. We're just backup."

Bernadette realized the gravity of what Melinda had said. This was all becoming real now. This was play-acting to Melinda's brother and his friends, but soon, this would be for real. She had to meet with Ace.

She crossed the large avenue and made her way back to school. She was mulling over in her mind what she'd need to do, how she'd need to act, when a strange sensation came over her.

As if she was being watched. Her grandfather had always told her to stop and glance behind her in the forest. Animals stalked the unaware. She stopped and turned. An old Chevy Malibu stopped down the street.

Bernadette stared hard at the car. She couldn't identify the occupants. But the car looked familiar. There'd been one just like it parked behind Gus's place on the reservation. It was gold with a black hard top.

She turned and walked faster. The Chevy revved its engine. It picked up speed. When it got close to her, it mounted the sidewalk, coming straight for her.

21

BERNADETTE DIVED OVER A SNOWBANK. The car careened off the bank, bounced back onto the road, and skidded to a stop. She looked up from the deep snow she'd landed in. The car backed up. A door opened.

She needed to run. The deep snow rose to her knees. She lunged from one step to another, coming to rest between two apartment buildings.

The car stopped. She couldn't see inside the darkened windows—instinct told her it had to be the Cardinal boys. She made her way at a slow run between the buildings. They opened onto an alleyway in the back.

She pulled the cell phone out of her backpack. If she called 9-1-1, how long would the police take to get here? As she powered up the phone, the car roared away, turning the corner. She knew it would come down the alleyway.

She put the phone away. Could she make it across the alley before the car? The engine's roar became louder. She ran from the shelter of the apartment buildings, through their parking lots, and made for the alley. The car had just entered the alley. It picked up speed, heading for her.

A high fence stood before her. The car raced towards her. She froze for a mere second. As the car approached, she grabbed an empty metal trashcan, heaved it at the car's windshield, and jumped up to grab the top of the fence. She threw one leg up and hoisted herself over. She dropped over the other side.

A big dog growled.

A large German shepherd stood before his doghouse. His growl deep, his ears back, his tail dropped. He wasn't happy Bernadette had appeared in his yard.

Bernadette stood up slowly. She let her hands fall to her side. There was no way back. She had to go forward. It meant through this large, upset dog. "I'm not here to hurt you," she said in a low, calm voice.

The dog barked. He bared his teeth. He moved closer. His body became rigid. An attack was imminent. She raised her voice, this time speaking in Dene, the language of her grandfather. "I said, I'm not here to hurt you. I will cause you no harm."

The dog's ears went up. It sat on its haunches and stared at Bernadette as if this person had just turned into an alien. Bernadette smiled. She continued speaking in Dene. "You have the spirit of the wolf in you. You are a brother to my people. Thank you for allowing me to travel through your yard."

She walked past the dog to the front of the house, found the gate, and made her way to the street. Voices yelled behind her, "Down dog, get down."

The dog barked at someone else who'd entered the yard. A male voiced screamed. "Let go of my leg. Damn it, somebody hit him, let go of my leg."

A lady yelled. "You boys leave my dog alone and get out of my yard. I've called the police. Hannibal, leave that boy alone."

Though she was shaking, she laughed. The Cardinal boys must have followed her over the fence. She did not know which boy the dog had bitten, but she didn't care. The dog had given her the best escape possible.

She cut through a parking lot and made her way back to school. Travis and his team walked out of the gym as she arrived.

"Hey, Bernadette," Travis said as he walked over, toweling himself off. "You get all your homework done in study hall?"

Bernadette shrugged, eyeing Travis's bulging chest glistening with sweat. "Oh, I got most of it done. Still, a few bits left..."

Travis swept her up in a big bear hug and kissed her forehead. "Good, 'cause when you're there, I know you're safe. I don't want anyone to mess with my little angel."

"Yep, that's me, all safe and sound," Bernadette said, sighing on the inside, knowing things like this would have her saying penance. If she ever got to confession.

She waited for Travis to come out of the shower and contemplated calling Officer Myers about the Cardinal boys chasing her. Bernadette realized she'd never really seen them.

But the car looked like the one parked out back at Gus's store. And the person's voice who screamed—it sounded like Stephen Cardinal.

She had a dilemma. If she called Myers about this, she'd have to make a report at the station. Travis would want to accompany her, which meant he'd know she'd snuck out of the school without him as her bodyguard. Shaking her head, she muttered, "*I really know how to complicate my life.*"

* * *

Stephen Cardinal screamed in pain in the back seat of the car, "Bastard dog bit me." He pulled up his pant leg. "I'm gonna get gangrene or something. I need a hospital."

Tommy shook his head from behind the wheel. "No way, man, we're going to the drugstore and get some antiseptic and a bandage. Who knows if the lady called the cops? Who knows what she did, they could've put one of those all point bulletins on us or something."

Peter sat in the passenger seat, shaking his head. "What the hell are you thinking? You tried to run her down in broad daylight. How many kinds of stupid are you, Stephen?"

"I saw an opportunity, and I took it, okay. Better than some coward ass like you, Peter. You keep telling us to play it safe, bide our time; well, I took action, okay. That's what warriors do," Stephen said.

"No, I don't remember no warrior chasing a girl in a car." Peter said. He turned to Tommy. "How about after you've doctored up our brave warrior back there, you drop me at the bus station? I'm about done with this."

Tommy pulled the car over to the curb. He looked at Peter, and his eyes narrowed. "You listen here, chickenshit, you're going nowhere. You're a Cardinal, part of our family, you ain't done 'til I say we're done. 'Cause I can make you disappear just like I'm going to do with Bernadette. You hear me?"

Peter said nothing; he stared out the car window. A mother walked by with her child holding her hand. The child looked at him and smiled. He couldn't force his mouth to smile back.

22

BERNADETTE PUT the kids to bed, waited until they fell asleep before she turned on the video the boys had given her.

Her mind had been bouncing around all the things she'd discussed with Melinda's brother and his friends. Could they pull this off? And her escape from the Cardinal boys—she felt like a cat with nine lives. How many had she used up?

She'd lied easily to Travis about being in study hall, and she hadn't told him about her encounter with the Cardinals. The lies made her life even more complicated.

She made herself tea and put in the first video. Fast-forwarding through *Goodfellas*, as she watched it before, she put in *Bad Lieutenant*, which she'd seen before as well. She held the *Debbie Does Dallas* in her hands, hesitated, and put it in the machine.

After watching it for an hour, it exhausted her. They had exposed her to the movie's language in the schoolyard. However, she learned a lot of new sex terms. They made her agitated. Her young mind now awash in images.

She shut the video off, changed into her gi, and began doing her training *katas*. Karate channeled her energy. Sexual thoughts pounded in her brain. She needed an outlet to calm herself down.

She started with her *katas*; the training moves she'd learned in the dojo, by progressing through low and high blocks, turns and kicks. She missed some moves. Her last sessions had been perfect.

She stopped, doing breath exercises to pull the power of *chi*, the breath towards her, expelling negative thoughts and bad *chi* away from her. After ten minutes, she felt better. One kata followed the other until she perfected them.

Covered in sweat, she drew a bath and stripped off her gi. She examined herself in the mirror. She turned seventeen in a week. Her body had developed at an exponential rate. Her breasts, legs and arms seemed in a contest to sprout the fastest.

Her breasts had grown in the past six months. Did they have a mind of their own? She'd secretly wanted to throw them a coming out party but never told her grandma or aunt. She thought they might not get the joke.

Bernadette still understood little about her sexuality. She had an attraction to boys, but still uncertain as to all the urges she had. Catholic's, had many taboos about sexuality. She wondered how the religion had survived with so many rules covering intercourse and masturbation.

Steam rose from the bath as she stepped in. She lay there, submerging herself in the tub, and thought about the sin of masturbation in the church. The priest and nuns preached masturbation was wrong. Because it was about your pleasure, and not for procreation.

They also deemed it to be adultery in your heart, and for the unwed, like Bernadette, this posed a problem. She didn't plan on being married for some time, so what to do with the pleasure center budding between her legs?

There would be the problem with confession at the church should she go this Sunday, but she might call it "unholy thoughts," the ultimate catch phrase for all Catholics.

The church called these "Venal Sins"; they were not mortal, but immoral, as in lack of judgment or losing their way along the path of righteousness.

Bernadette reasoned in her young mind, if Catholics told the God's honest truth about the riotous thoughts they had, the priest would run screaming from the confessional booth.

She let these thoughts drift around her mind as her hands massaged her tired legs, knees and made their way to her thighs. Her fingers did small circles around her inner thigh and rested on her pubic bone. She let her fingers get caught in her newly grown pubic hair, using some soap to pretend she was washing the area.

The soap came loose in her hands and floated to the surface. Her hands remained there, frozen in place—her little spot of forbidden pleasure.

She began a slow massage and probed deeper. She groaned. Her eyelids closed as she kept going; this time she was going all the way. She reasoned the priests would never deny this if they knew how good it felt.

As Bernadette hit climax she moaned, "Please forgive me, Father, for I have sinned."

The door to the apartment opened. Bernadette raised herself out of the tub and grabbed her towel. Had the Cardinals boys found her?

She peeked out the door to watch her aunt enter the apartment. "Hey, Aunt Mary, you scared me. I didn't expect your back."

Aunt Mary stood in the darkened hallway. She moved into the kitchen's light. A bandage covered the left side of her face.

"What happened?"

Aunt Mary walked to the kitchen table. She sat down, letting herself drop into the chair like one who'd been in a prizefight and got the crap beat out of them. "I quit my job."

Bernadette came to stand by her aunt's side. "What? Why'd you quit your job? Did Ace come after you again?" she asked.

Aunt Mary broke into sobs. "Yeah... he grabbed me again behind the bar... I slapped him... he hit me." She looked up at Bernadette. "I can't take it there anymore. It's not worth the tips."

"I'm going to get the bastard," Bernadette said. Her hands curled into her karate fists. She envisioned herself pounding on Ace until his face looked like hamburger.

"No, you'll do nothing. Remember, I'm a barmaid, and an Indian from the reservation. I don't matter, and you don't matter in this town either." Aunt Mary stared up at Bernadette. "Don't you get it? We Indians and half breeds like you, we mean nothing to these people. They get to beat on us, spit on us, and no one gives a shit."

"You're wrong, Aunt Mary, I give a shit, and so do you, and we're the ones who matter," Bernadette said. She sat beside Aunt Mary and put her arms around her. "We matter, because we matter to each other. The others can go to hell."

"Is it that simple in your world?" Aunt Mary asked.

Bernadette stared at her aunt; should she tell her she planned to set up Ace and turn him over to his gang leader? She couldn't do it now, not in her aunt's fragile state. She got up from the table and opened the freezer to take out some ice cream.

"Yeah, pretty much, and hey, how about some ice cream?" Bernadette asked as she brought out two bowls and some chocolate chip swirl.

She filled two bowls with massive scoops and sat down beside her aunt. "Here's how I look at it. You needed to move anyway. It's a crap job, Aunt Mary."

Aunt Mary shook her head, "Sure it was crap, but it paid well. We'll have to cancel our new apartment." She dropped her ice cream by her side. "God, I screwed us up, didn't I? I brought that enormous piece of shit in here. You threw him out, now he's out to get us."

"What do you mean?"

"He's getting to you by slapping me around," Aunt Mary said.

"Really, are you serious?"

"Yeah." Aunt Mary turned to Bernadette. "Ace said he's sending a message to you from Susie—and suddenly he backhanded me." Her shoulders shook in sobs.

Bernadette put her arm around Aunt Mary and rested her aunt's head on her shoulder. "What if I said I have a plan to take Ace and Susie down?"

Aunt Mary sniffled, blew her nose, and looked at Bernadette. "What kinda plan? Are the police after him? Are they going to arrest him?" She sat up, her body shaking. "You can't have me lay assault charges. My god, Ace would kill me, and do the same to you and my kids."

"No, nothing like that," Bernadette said, giving her aunt a reassuring hug. "I heard talk from Officer Myers they've got a little surprise up their sleeve for Ace, and pretty soon he'll be history, and so will Susie. Now, eat your ice cream." She picked up her aunt's ice cream and handed it to her.

"Do you always view life as positive and sunny?" Aunt Mary asked, putting a big scoop of ice cream in her mouth and letting it melt.

"No, not always, but it's better than trying to always scrape the shit off your shoe. Now, eat your ice cream, get a good night's sleep. Tomorrow you'll find a new job."

"But we'll need to give notice to the Goodhues we can't take their apartment."

"Nope, not happening. You'll find a proper job. There's a bunch out there. Stop thinking you're no good, Aunt Mary. You're one hell of hard-working lady who's let the world tell her she not good enough." She shook her spoon at her. "Time for a change."

Aunt Mary dabbed a Kleenex over her nose and smiled. "When did you become the adult in this place?"

Bernadette grinned, took a big mouthful of ice cream, and wondered if she really was as good as the story she told Aunt Mary. She needed to pull off a miracle to get it done. She wondered if the price of the miracle might be too high.

23

Bernadette felt refreshed the next morning. She realized the reaction stemmed from her illicit sexual release in the bathtub last night. It tugged at her conscience, but she let it go. She decided not to be guilty about something so good—especially that good.

She wondered for a moment what business the Catholic Church had in her sexual life, and then she dropped the thought as her phone rang.

"How's it going, Bernadette? Did you watch the tapes I gave you?" Jason asked.

"Yeah, I can say I'm a dirty girl now—is that what you wanted?"

"No, we want you to play the part to get Ace's attention."

"I think anyone who flashes boobs at him will get his attention."

"You're on to something. How's your aunt doing, by the way? I heard she got slapped around by Ace last night."

Bernadette stood in the kitchen on her own. Her aunt and the kids. She dropped her voice to a whisper. "How did you know about it?"

"Craig and Chad scoped out the tavern last night, to get the lay of the place. They witnessed Ace hitting your aunt."

"Why didn't they intervene?" Bernadette asked.

"Craig and Chad are pretty lightweight, I mean as nerds go, they're in the shallow end of the pool. They'd have been something extra for Ace to beat up." Jason said.

Bernadette sighed. "Yeah, I know what you mean, but they might have filed an assault charge."

"Sure, and he'd be out tomorrow, and we still got him dealing drugs at your school, and your aunt would have to testify," Jason said. "I don't think this is where we wanted to go with this. Remember, we want to get rid of him."

Bernadette looked towards the bathroom where the girls made splashing sounds. "You're right. An assault charge just brings my aunt into it. You did the right thing. Craig and Chad would have been soft punching bags for him."

"Sorry about what happened to your aunt. Chad and Craig found it hard to watch. But the bar manager did nothing about it except ask Ace to leave," Jason said.

"When do we go after this bastard?" Bernadette asked.

"How about tonight?"

Bernadette's heart did a flip. Her breathing stopped. Tonight? Was she ready for tonight? "Sure... where and when?"

"The tavern where you aunt worked. We understand she quit, so you won't be running into her. You need to dress sexy. Make him want you. We'll provide the dialogue. Got it?"

"Yeah, I got it," Bernadette said as she closed her phone.

Her aunt walked in the kitchen toweling her hair and looked at the cell phone. "Where'd you get the phone?"

"Oh, this?" Bernadette said, holding up the phone. "Travis lent it to me; he wanted me to be safe in case the Cardinal boys come after me."

"Good, I'm glad that's where you got it from, because at your school, the drug dealers carry cell phones," Aunt Mary said.

"Yeah, how about that? I've got some stuff going on tonight. You mind picking up the kids after school?"

"Sure, no problem. I'm going out to search for a new job today and pick up my last pay cheque from the bar, but I'll be here. You going to hang out with your cool new friends?"

Bernadette broke into a winning, lying smile. "Yeah, some of my cool new friends. I'll call you if I'm going to be home past ten."

She slipped by her aunt and continued to the bedroom. They all shared the closet, but none of them had many clothes. She rummaged through her aunt's working clothes, since they were about the same size—she found a tight-fitting, open neck black blouse and short black skirt and a black lace bra. They'd be perfect. She snagged some high heel boots and stuffed them into her backpack.

The door to the bedroom opened as Bernadette closed her backpack. Not a moment too soon. She breezed by her aunt with a kiss on her cheek. "See you tonight."

The kids stood at the door whining they needed to get outside before they overheated in their winter gear. Bernadette ushered them out the door. A blast of cold air smacked them in the face. Winter had returned with full force.

Snow covered the sidewalks. The city crews barely kept the major streets clear. Car tires made a crunching sound on the snow as they compacted the snow into ice on the roadway.

Travis waited at the corner for her. The kids said hi and marched ahead with their heads tucked into their hoods to avoid the biting cold.

"You okay today?" Travis asked.

"Yeah, I'm fine, why'd you ask?"

"You seem radiant this morning. Did you win the lottery or something?"

Bernadette's face turned a deep shade of red, her eyes dropped to the ground. "Hey, can't a girl just be happy to be alive with her favorite guy?"

"Sorry, it's just, I've never seen you so..."

"Happy?"

"Ah, yeah, I guess that's it."

Bernadette shook her head. She did not know orgasms showed from the night before. She'd be more careful from now on.

They walked together in silence for a while. Their breath steamed into the air and mingled, and they held each other close as the snow crunched under their feet. Bernadette realized her episode in the bathtub had unleashed a wave of impure thoughts of things she wanted to do with Travis.

Her body pressed close to him. His thigh bumped into her, and she almost moaned. *My god, girl, she thought, you've become a mess of hormones.*

School was a blur; she'd set her phone to vibrate and hoped Jason wouldn't call during a class. They had a pop quiz in French she didn't remember finishing and wondered if she'd passed when she handed it in.

When school finished, she told Travis she needed to go to the dojo to do some work on her karate moves. He walked to the karate school with her as she wove a web of lies that she didn't need him after the karate finished. She told Travis she'd walk home with other students.

She waved to them, and they waved back from inside the dojo, which made it seem they were in on her lie. Travis smiled, kissed her, and left. Bernadette felt very alone at that moment. She'd lied to get away from Travis, to help trap Ace, but who was going to help her?

The other students moved in unison with their practice as Bernadette walked in. She changed into her gi and began working on her yellow belt moves.

Sensei stood there for a while and watched her. When she'd finished the *katas* he said, "You move with tension. Is there something bothering you?"

Bernadette whirled around to face him. "Sorry, sensei," she said, bowing to him. "I didn't notice you there."

"You do not seem to notice much. Your mind is clouded, your moves are stilted," sensei said.

"Yes, sensei," Bernadette said with another bow. He read her like a book.

"Stop doing the katas and practice karate breathing until your mind is clear," sensei said and walked away.

"Oss," Bernadette said with a low bow. If her sensei sensed her troubled mind, how would she hide it from Ace?

She moved to the side of the dojo and practiced breathing by expelling her breath as she extended her arms and inhaling from deep in her abdomen as she pulled her arms in. A calmness came over her after a few minutes.

She remembered a time when hunting Elk with her grandfather; they came across a grizzly bear and her cubs on the trail. The big grizzly had risen on its hind legs, roaring a warning.

It had terrified Bernadette. Her grandfather spoke to the bear in Dene, his native language. The bear dropped to the ground and walked away with her cubs.

When Bernadette asked her grandfather what he'd said to the bear, he said, "I told her she didn't need to be afraid of us, but if she charged, I'd kick her ass."

Her grandfather's memory flooded over her. A small tear formed at her eye as she finished her breathing. It reminded her of the inner strength needed. She slipped into the change room and found a message from Jason on her phone.

She dialed him back. "We're outside in a white Town and Country van. Did you bring something sexy?" Jason asked.

"Yeah, I did; I've got it with me."

"Good, get dressed and get out here. "

The school had one private dressing room in the change room. Bernadette pulled the door shut and took out her aunt's clothes. She'd never worn a short skirt, nor the blouse with the plunging neckline. Could she go through with this?

She stripped off her gi and folded the clothing items with reverence into the small gym bag she'd brought. A small shudder went through her as she looked at the clothes she was about to wear. These were actor's clothes; they required her to assume an identity the moment she put them on.

She wiggled into the skirt and realized just how short it was. She was taller than her aunt. It exposed her thighs. Then, she saw to her horror the black lace bra was missing. It must have fallen out of pack. Her sports bra wouldn't go with the sexy look.

She pulled off her sports bra and put the deep cut blouse over her bare skin. It made her feel exposed. *"Yeah, you look sexy. Too sexy,"* she whispered to herself, looking in the mirror.

"What was that?" a voice asked from outside the change room.

"Oh, nothing, I was just talking to myself—about nothing in particular. Sorry," Bernadette answered back in confusion.

Her face had gone red with embarrassment, staring at herself in the mirror. The skirt exposed her thighs, and the blouse was showing her breasts as if they were in a contest. How was she going to pull this off?

When she'd attended Catholic schools, cleavage was a sin for girls. The nuns had admonished any girl who'd walked the hallways with even one button undone, and God forbid the girl who wore a tight blouse who presumed to show she had breasts. Their blouses billowed in front to hide their breasts from prying eyes. They were the next best things to a nun's habit.

Here was Bernadette in her full bloom of youth, showing off her breasts to the world in this outfit. Were there enough Hail Marys to get out of the hell she'd be in for this?

She sighed, pulled on her aunt's boots that were too tight and hurt like hell, and threw her parka overtop. She walked from the change room with the other girls staring at her.

"Wow," one girl exclaimed. "You must have a hot date tonight."

Bernadette smiled at the girl. "No, I'm trying out for a part in a hooker movie."

"I think you'll nail the part," the girl said.

Bernadette shot out the door as fast as she could. God help her if sensei saw her wearing this outfit. The van was half a block down the street. By the time she got to it, her legs felt frozen.

A side door opened. A blast of welcoming warm air greeted her. Jason pulled her in and motioned her to sit in one of the big captain's chairs. The van had plush leather seats with thick carpet and wood paneling. This thing must have cost Melinda's mother a pile of dough, Bernadette thought.

Craig sat in the driver's seat; Melinda was in the last seat, and Chad hunched over an expanse of electronic equipment with impressive blinking lights in the center.

"What's all this?" Bernadette asked.

Chad looked up from his console. "Consider this as the command deck of the starship *Enterprise*." He swept his hand over the console. "Here is the latest in GPS tracking technology as provided by the university engineering department, the latest in listening devices from our computer lab, and *voila...*" He produced a big round wad of brown one hundred-dollar bills. "We have your walking around money, courtesy of the faculty of business administration and their high-tech laser printer."

Bernadette looked into the back row. "Melinda, you didn't have to come on this."

"Are you kidding? I'm just as pumped as these guys. I told you I'd be at your back," Melinda said. "And besides, I brought a makeup bag I borrowed from my mother."

"Makeup? What am I going to do with makeup? I thought the sexy clothes would do the job."

"Oh, goodness no, girl, we're going to glam you up tonight, throw on some perfume and make you and your cash irresistible," Melinda said.

"Okay," Bernadette said, "I'm in your hands." She pulled off her parka, revealing her aunt's outfit.

Craig was about to pull the van away from the curb. He looked in the rearview mirror and caught sight of Bernadette. "Oh, my God."

Jason looked at Craig and then back at Bernadette. "Wow—I'd say you've got the look." Jason turned to face the road. He lifted his head and said, "Hey, Melinda, your girlfriend is going to rock tonight."

Melinda came forward to the chair beside Bernadette. "Ah, you don't think it's maybe a little too sexy? I'd say you're bordering on provocative. You think he might want to try something?"

Bernadette shook her head. "It's all I found from my aunt's." She leaned forward to Melinda. "I lost the bra that matched this."

Melinda rolled her eyes. She looked up front. "Hey, Craig, you mind watching the road? There's nothing to see back here."

"Sorry," Craig said, as he glued his eyes back to the road instead of Bernadette, his face turning red.

Jason laughed from the front. "If you can get Craig's attention, Ace shouldn't be a problem. I think you've passed the first test."

"Are we heading to the tavern to meet Ace?" Bernadette asked.

Chad raised his head from his computer. "Yes, we installed a tracking device on Ace's car last night. He arrived at the tavern about a half hour ago."

Jason turned in his seat. "Here are the talking points. You want to buy eight balls, nothing smaller. The buy is ten large and you flash him your wad, understand?"

"Yeah... I understand... ten large," Bernadette said, as she locked eyes with Melinda. This was beyond anything she'd experienced. Her mouth felt dry. She gulped some water from a bottle and fought to breathe.

"You okay?" Melinda asked, reaching over and taking her hand.

Bernadette managed a smile. "I'm nervous, you know, the stage lights and all."

"You'll be fine," Melinda said.

The van pulled up in front of the tavern. Melinda pulled out a bag and applied makeup to Bernadette.

"I didn't know you were into cosmetics," Bernadette said.

"I'm not, I used to do the makeup for school plays for the actors," Melinda said.

"Which plays?"

"I did *The Wizard of Oz*. The audience loved my Wicked Witch of the West," Melinda said.

"Great," Bernadette said. "Just don't make me resemble Dorothy —or Toto."

"Do you know what you're going to do when you enter the tavern?" Jason asked.

Bernadette looked at Jason with her now heavy-lined eyes and well rouged cheeks and full lips. "I'm going to take control and kick his ass. Now, what about the tape recorder I'm going to wear? The wire thing—how do you attach it to me?"

Chad smiled. "Oh, so nineties technology. You're talking with the guys who do future-tech. When Craig and I checked the place last night, we noticed which table Ace likes. When he hassled your aunt, we attached a radio transmitter under his table."

Craig looked from the driver's seat. "He can frisk you all he wants, he's gonna find nothing." He raised his eyebrows, looking at Bernadette. She stared back at him, her eyes squinting to pull him into full target range. He turned back around.

"I want you to take your phone and place it on the table in front of you. It's going to be on," Jason said. "We'll have dialed you into my phone so we have instant communication."

"So you can come running to my aide or call the cops?" Bernadette asked. Her eyes searched Jason's handsome face. He looked away. She knew the answer. These three guys wouldn't be able to do much to defend her against Ace. She was on her own in there.

Melinda gave Bernadette a small handbag and a weak smile. "Go get him, girl."

Bernadette stuffed the fake one hundred dollars bills into a gold handbag Melinda provided for a prop and took her phone from Jason once he'd dialed in his number. She climbed out of the van, careful not to fall on the ice as she made her way across the street.

She smelled the tavern from a distance as she approached. It reeked of stale beer and cigarettes. It brought back memories of her parents and their singing gigs in places even more run down than this one.

She stood before the doors. The murmur of male voices soaked in alcohol came from the other side. Taking one last deep breath, she pushed the doors open.

The tavern was dark; it took a moment to let her eyes grow accustomed to the low light. She felt his presence before she saw him. Ace stared at her from a table a few metres away.

24

SHOW TIME, Bernadette muttered to herself. She unzipped her parka, took four strides to Ace's table, and threw her parka over a chair. She pulled a chair out from the table, moved it close to him, and sat down.

"Hello, Ace," she said, leaning forward and making sure he caught an eyeful of her best features.

Ace looked stunned. He stared at her face, then her breasts, back to her face, and then he focused on her breasts. "Who the hell are you?" he asked.

"I'm up here, Ace." Bernadette motioned with her hands for Ace to focus on her eyes.

"Well... yeah, but I'm just checking your assets."

"I'm glad I impress you, but I'm here to talk business, not to give you a peep show."

Ace looked up at Bernadette, stared hard at her for a minute. "Wait a minute, ain't I seen you before?"

"Maybe, I get around."

"No, I don't forget pretty little things like you... I remember..." Ace said. His eyes narrowed, and his fist clenched. "You're the little bitch threw me out of Mary's apartment."

Panic swept over her. She needed to distract him or her game was up. "Yeah, that was me. Why would I share you with my aunt?" She moved a hand across the table. "Ace, you have me, you won't have the time or energy for anyone else. You catch my drift?"

"What kinda game you playing at?"

Bernadette sat back for a second. He was fading; she needed to pull him back in, get his interest. "Look, Ace, I understand you've got some serious weight in eight balls. I got serious cash. That makes us compatible. Don't you?"

"What kind a cash?"

Bernadette put her purse on the table and opened it enough for him to see. "I got five large in here, and another ten large for later this week. Serious enough for you?"

"Where you get that kinda cash?"

"None of your business. You want to do serious business or do little gram shit with dumb ass Susie? Is she the one you're humping right now? I bet she can't make the moves like I can. You ain't never had it, mister, until you had an athletic girl like me ride you like a stallion. You get me?"

Ace leaned back in his chair and spread his legs. His posture showed control—not fear. He wore gray sweat pants stuffed into big black boots. A thick plaid shirt flopped over the pants that looked like it had never seen a washing machine.

"How you going to move the stuff? I never saw you dealing around the school. You got some kinda distribution?"

Bernadette snapped the purse shut and threw it beside her parka. "I got the best distribution in town. You know all those big wrestling boys, well, they distribute for me, and they go from one school to another to do matches. Best cover in the whole damn city."

"How come I'm hearing this now? Susie would have told me if crystal was being distributed in your school? She mentioned no competitors," Ace said.

Bernadette shook her head. "Well, one thing you gotta realize, Ace, Susie is pretty stupid. She only sees what's in front of her—no, I'm wrong, she don't even see that most of the time." Bernadette placed her hands on the table. "I'm not interested in my high school, I'm interested in all the high schools, and then I'll move on to the colleges and the university. I can lock up this town in the next month if you can supply me."

"You're bullshitting me. You're probably wearing a wire, and here to get me back for slapping your aunt around," Ace said. "Yeah, you got an axe you wanna grind and I'm the one you wanna grind it on."

"Ace, I couldn't give a shit about my aunt, she's a dumb ass, been working in this shit hole for too long. She gave me a couch to sleep on while I got my act together, and it's excellent cover. You think I gotta wire, you can frisk me, but if you run one hand up my dress and try to grab my crotch or grab a boob, I'll break your fucking hand."

Ace leaned forward. "If you're screwing with me, I'll make sure you die slowly—you hear me?"

"Yeah, you're a tough guy, but a poor, tough guy. You want to shift serious merchandise, I can make it happen. You want to sit in this shit hole all day drinking cheap rum and coke all day, knock yourself out."

Ace pushed his rum and coke away from him. Suddenly the drink was offensive. He stood up from the table, towering over Bernadette.

"I don't need to take this crap from you, little bitch."

Bernadette didn't move. She sat back in her chair, letting her breathing relax. She crossed her legs and let her eyes move slowly up his enormous frame, letting him know she saw him there, but he wasn't a threat.

"We'll take a lot a shit when someone's providing us with a golden opportunity. You either want to deal with me and my cash and take a little sass..." She raised one eyebrow and smiled. "Or you keep dealing grams from your car. It's easy to stay small time."

Ace's mind worked over her words and the money he could make. "Okay, kid, how about you and me go in the back for a quick stand up screw? We could seal the deal and all."

Bernadette stood up; she was inches from him; she felt his body heat, smelled his offensive odor. "No thanks, Ace. You need a bath real bad, and I got better things to do." She handed him a piece of paper. "Here's my cell number. You call me when you got sixty nice eight balls put together, and I'll meet you with the cash."

"Ah, c'mon, it'll only take a minute," Ace said, raising his hands towards Bernadette's breast. His eyes looked mean, like the night he'd been in her aunt's apartment.

Bernadette threw up her forearms and deflected his hands. She kicked him hard in the shin. Ace's face exploded in pain. She threw a punch into his solar plexus. He doubled over. She guided him back into his chair with her hands on his throat.

"Now, Ace, I warned you, any advances on me without my permission would cause serious injury."

He made three quick nods. Bernadette's hands constricted his vocal cords.

"You be a nice boy, bring me some good quality merchandise, no shit mind you, and I give you a little action as a reward. I like rough and kinky guys like you, but on my own terms. You catch my drift?" Bernadette said with a smile as she released his throat.

"I got it," Ace said in a hoarse whisper.

Bernadette grabbed her parka, threw it over her shoulders, and surveyed the bar. The patrons were staring at her. The place had gone quiet. No one had ever taken on Ace. This pretty young lady had walked in and stepped on the big thug and made him heel.

"Show's over, guys," Bernadette said with a wink to the other men in the bar. They looked uncomfortable, as if someone had just beaten their favorite prizefighter. She sauntered out slowly, knowing every man had his eyes rivetted to her ass.

The cold outside snapped her out of her act. She came crashing back down to reality, feeling nausea in her stomach and chills running up and down her body. Her forehead broke out in a sweat. The reality of what she had done in the tavern sank in.

The van door opened. Jason and Melinda pulled her into the van and sat her in a chair.

"Wow. What a show you put on in there," Jason said. "My god, girl, I'd give you an Oscar."

"Did he buy it?"

"Bought it, are you kidding me?" Chad said. "You had me and Craig here with hard-ons. Damn, girl, you had it going on in there, you'd make a fortune doing phone sex."

"Chad, you're an idiot," Melinda said.

Bernadette shrugged. "You told me to take control, so that's what I went with—what's our next move?"

Chad held up a cassette tape. "We take this and drop it off to Carl Hoffer, the Devil's Undertakers big daddy."

"Is it incriminating enough?" Bernadette asked.

"He said he didn't know about any competitors. I'd say it's pretty plain. He also implicated Susie," Chad said.

Bernadette hugged her parka around her; suddenly she felt a chill. "So, we mail it to him, send it by courier? What's the plan?"

"How about we drop it off to him? The clubhouse for the Devil's Undertakers is a twenty-minute drive from here. We put it in a small envelope, put it in their mailbox, and bingo, we make Ace disappear faster than a card trick," Jason said.

Melinda and Bernadette rolled their eyes at Jason's sick humor. They sat next to each other as Craig started the van and drove towards the clubhouse.

"Good job," Melinda said, looking at Bernadette.

Bernadette looked at Melinda and gave her thumbs up. Deep inside, she realized this night wasn't over. Nothing would be simple about tonight. There was a lingering tension in her gut telling her she'd set things in motion. The outcome wasn't clear, but she felt like she had awakened the black wolf. She heard a faint howl in the back of her mind—she broke into a sweat.

25

BERNADETTE UNZIPPED HER JACKET, the cold bit into her like a knife. Bernadette's heart pounded. For a moment, she closed her eyes, took a breath and relaxed. She needed all her strength from within.

The gate buzzed. The sound was like a gunshot in the stillness. "Come in."

Her legs pushed her forward with her mind screaming at her to turn around. She forced air into her lungs to calm down while every part of her had become elevated into flight mode.

A metal door opened. She stepped in. The entryway opened into a large room with overstuffed armchairs and table lamps. The floors were hardwood with throw rugs. Paintings of motorcycles adorned the wall.

Bernadette noticed the paintings in oil and acrylic with solid wood frames. She'd expected a grimy place filled with beer bottles and takeout food containers. This place was nice; it smelled of fresh paint and a hint of... lavender?

A man stood by the door with a suspicious stare on his face. He looked mid-forties with a long goatee streaked with gray, his long hair tied into a neat ponytail. He wore clean jeans with a white t-shirt and leather vest. "Take off you shoes," he said.

Bernadette sat on the padded hallway bench and removed her boots. She felt smaller, more defenseless. If she had to run, she never make it in bare feet, but then, she'd never get out the heavy door.

"I have to frisk you for weapons," the man said. "Take off your jacket and place your hands on the wall."

Bernadette rolled her eyes. "What is with you guys, you want to put your hands on me?"

The man pointed to a sign on the wall. "It's the rule. I check you for weapons or I eject you out the door."

Bernadette looked at the sign on the wall: *We frisk everyone for weapons. No exceptions.*

She handed the man her jacket. He placed it on a wooden hanger in the closet. She turned and placed her hands on the wall. "By the way, I don't need a massage."

"I'd have to frisk my mother if she came in here," the man said.

He patted his hands over her upper body, then ran his hands up her legs. His hands were soft, almost soothing. Bernadette shook her head; how could some old guy with a ponytail activate her bloody libido?

"Follow me," the man said.

Bernadette padded behind him in her bare feet. He was wearing leather slippers. They crossed the living room and went down a hall. They passed the kitchen. Music was playing. The soft melody of the Eagles tune *Take It Easy* was playing. Roast chicken wafted into the air with a hint of garlic and rosemary. A man wearing an apron stirred a pot in the kitchen, rocking in tune to the music. Bernadette thought she'd dropped into a fraternity house for old bikers.

The hall ended at a door. He opened the door and motioned for her to go inside. The room was dark, and a man sat behind a desk. A desk lamp shone in her face. She couldn't make his features.

"Sit down," the man at the desk commanded.

Bernadette sat down. "Mr. Hoffer?"

"Yeah. And you are?" Hoffer asked. He had a rough voice that sounded like his vocal cords had run over gravel.

"Let's call me a concerned citizen," Bernadette said.

Hoffer chuckled. "We don't get a lot of those here—what's your angle?"

"I have information that one your club members, you call him Ace, is dealing drugs at a high school, he's using someone named Susie Ferguson and her gang to distribute."

"That's a serious offense to our code—you got proof?"

Bernadette pulled the tape recorder from her jacket pocket and slid it over to him. His hand reached out and picked it up.

"You want to play it?" Bernadette asked.

"No, I'll take your word for it. I assume you tried to set him up?" Hoffer asked, "Did he go for it?"

"Yeah, I'm to meet him this week with ten large to buy a bunch of eight balls," Bernadette said. She couldn't believe how easily the lingo was coming to her.

"You with the cops?" Hoffer asked.

"No," Bernadette said all too quickly. "I did this on my own. I don't want to see drugs in our school." Her heart raced at the new lie she'd told. She couldn't tell him it was to get Ace away from her aunt and Susie off her back.

Hoffer was silent. A large antique clock ticked in the room's corner. Bernadette stared into the desk light, wondering if he was going to buy her story or if she would not leave this place alive. Even with the hardwood floors and soft lighting, these were still drug-dealing bikers.

"Okay, kid, leave it with me. I'll make sure Ace and his people are no longer a problem to your school," Hoffer said.

Bernadette breathed a sigh of relief. "Thank you so much, Mr. Hoffer—"

"You can call me Carl."

"Thanks, Carl—really great of you. I really appreciate it, and my school thanks you—"

"Okay, I get it. Now get out of here, I have to select some wine for the roast chicken dinner. These guys don't know the difference between Chablis and a Sauvignon Blanc," Hoffer said.

Bernadette got up to leave.

"Oh, one more thing," Hoffer said

"What's that?"

"If you're ever looking for work when you hit eighteen, we pay good money for escorts. We have a great dental plan."

Bernadette blushed. "Well, thanks, Mr. Hoffer... but I think I'll be looking for something a bit more... let's say mainstream when I finish school."

"Okay, but you got some excellent assets, young lady, you could put them to use," Hoffer said.

"Thanks, I've been told that, thank you very much," Bernadette gushed as she walked out the door.

The ponytail man was standing at the door when she left the room. He led her back to the front door. She pulled on her boots, and ponytail man helped her with her jacket and ushered her out the door with a nod.

All her fears about dealing with the bike gang had vanished. They were nice guys; well, nice for drug dealing pimps, but nice all the same. Had that really happened?

She was humming a tune when she turned the corner of the narrow laneway and ran into Susie.

26

SUSIE STARED AT HER. It took her a few seconds to realize it was Bernadette. "What the hell you doing here?"

Bernadette swallowed hard. Her mind raced for an answer. "Ah... just doing some canvassing for Christmas charities... kinda getting a jump on the season..."

"Bullshit," Susie said. Her eyes traveled up and down Bernadette, taking in her short skirt and boots. "What're you up to, bitch?"

Bernadette cocked her head to one side. "None of your business, now, get out of my way. I have things to do."

Susie took a step closer. "Not going to happen." She was panting. Her breath rose into the air.

Bernadette moved her feet into her karate stance. A subtle move, right foot forward, turned in, left foot straight. Her knees bent slightly. She became rooted to the earth.

"I don't want to fight you," Bernadette said. She raised her hands, palms facing out and close to her chest.

"Yeah, course you don't. You ain't got your wrestling boys here to get your back. It's just you and me. Sure, you don't want to fight. But that's what's going to happen. You're going to fight, and I'm going to beat the hell out of you," Susie said. Her breath shrouded her from view.

Bernadette stood still. She saw Susie's eyes; her peripheral vision took in Susie's hands, arms, and feet. She'd trained in the dojo for weeks in combat, but this was real. Could she do it?

"Fighting solves nothing," Bernadette said.

"Maybe not for you—'cause you lose—solves everything for me," Susie said. She stepped closer.

Bernadette saw Susie's right shoulder move back. She took in a breath, let it out, and let the tension flow from her body. It was up to Susie to make the first move.

Susie exploded with a right hook. Bernadette's left arm came up in a sweeping block. Susie's fist glanced off Bernadette's arm. Her force carried her forward.

Bernadette's right fist corkscrewed up like a missile and landed under Susie's chin—she fell backwards, landing hard on the snow. Bernadette stood back to wait for Susie's next move.. She rolled over to her side and ran her hand over her jaw..

"Lucky hit," Susie said. Her breath rose higher into the night air.

Bernadette saw her anger. She needed to move her emotion up a notch, "I have lots more moves like that one. If you stay down, I'll leave you alone."

"Bullshit, lucky punch..." Susie dropped her head, breath streaming from her. She lurched forward, arms wide, head down, and came at Bernadette in a tackling position; she looked like a raging bull.

Bernadette waited. When Susie charged her, she stepped aside. She threw a punch into her side and put her right leg into Susie's legs. Susie went flying into a snowdrift.

"Damn you, bitch," Susie sputtered, pulling herself out of the snow. "I'm going to kill you. You hear me? I'm going to break every bone in your body and stuff you in a garbage can." She shook the snow off her like a dog,

"I don't want to hurt you, Susie," Bernadette said. She raised her palms up again. This was a classic fighting stance: it gave her multiple moves and didn't look threatening.

"That's fine," Susie said, breathing heavier, "you keep that in mind as I beat you to death." She raised her fists. "I give you credit, girl, you've learned some moves, but now, I know what you got, and I'm going to bring the pain."

Susie came at her slow—her fists in a boxer's stance. Bernadette had never faced a boxer before. She tracked Susie's eyes, trying to see which way she'd throw a punch. Susie feinted with her right, Bernadette threw a block—Susie threw a left jab into her ribs. Bernadette collapsed on the ground.

"There you go. That's the Bernadette I know. The one on the ground with me standing over her. Now, I'm going to crush your ass. You get me, bitch, you're going to know pain."

Bernadette kneeled on the ground, winded. Her stomach was in a knot. She couldn't let it happen again this way. She kept her head up, watching Susie's next move.

Susie raised her foot to stomp Bernadette's head. Bernadette grabbed her foot with both hands, twisting it and pushing away with all her strength. Susie fell onto her side. Bernadette leaped at Susie. She landed on Susie with her elbow and all her weight—Susie's ribs made a crunching sound. A large plume of air accompanied the oomph noise from Susie. Bernadette fell back on her knees and landed a punch to Susie's head. Susie's' head rolled over to the side. It was lights out.

Bernadette got up and dusted the snow off. She stood over Susie's unconscious body. Her breath came in a light stream, gently flowing into the cold air, as if the bull had been subdued.

"I lied Susie, I wanted to fight you. I wanted to kick your ass. And you're right—I do feel better. Thanks." Bernadette walked down the alley to the van.

Melinda was waiting, biting her lower lip. "What happened, Bernadette, what took you so long?"

Bernadette collapsed into the big chair. "I had to turn down a job offer and take out some trash." She smiled at Melinda. "Hoffer said he's going to take care of Ace and Susie. It's done."

"Excellent," Jason said. He turned to Craig. "I say we plot a course for pizza."

Bernadette sat back in the chair as the big van rolled through the winter's night. She'd met with two adversaries and laid them low. But would they stay down?

27

BERNADETTE DREAMED about white wolves and black wolves circling each other during the night. She woke up on the couch in a cold sweat. Her aunt walked into the kitchen and looked at her.

"Bad dream?" she asked.

"Yeah, I ate too much pizza last night."

"You got in pretty late, did you enjoy your time with your friends?"

"Real good, just too much pizza," Bernadette said, heading for the bathroom. She locked the door and ran the shower. The hot water was nice, and she'd love to stay longer if it wasn't for the pounding on the door of her little cousins. She came out of the bathroom and looked out the window.

A winter storm had blown in overnight. The wind was howling at the window. Snow crystals bounced and sounded like the fingers clawing on the panes.

Her stomach had a strange feeling, not hunger, not nausea—it was fear. The sharp whistle from the tea kettle startled her. A sense of foreboding gripped her.

Perhaps it was a delayed reaction from being so close to Ace. His smell, no matter how long she showered, still lingered in her nostrils.

How long would it take for Hoffer to get to Ace? What if he learned of her plan and came after her, or Aunt Mary and the kids? And what about Susie, she'd beaten her last night? Would Susie be out with her gang looking for revenge?

As she pulled out a knife to butter her toast, she noticed the carving knife there. Should she take it with her? Back on the reservation, her grandfather had her carry a hunting knife and a short throwing axe. He'd taught her to be accurate within ten metres—she was deadly at five. "If you're inside three meters, throw with force, one spin, and the axe will hit the target," Grandfather had said.

A throwing knife was the same, but it depended on the handle's weight. Bernadette picked up the carving knife. The handle was light. "*Piece of crap,*" she muttered.

"What did you say?" Aunt Mary asked.

"Ah—nothing," Bernadette said, putting the knife back in the drawer. She pulled herself together and got ready for school.

The minute she walked out the door and saw Travis wasn't waiting for her, she sensed something was wrong. He always called if he couldn't come. *The storm,* she said to herself, *it must be the storm.*

She doubted if anyone would try to harass her or attack her in this weather, half the school wouldn't show up for class. It was just -15C with a twenty-kilometer wind chill. What the hell, what sissies were they?

Bernadette trudged through the drifts, dropped her cousins off at school, and made her way to class. There were few students there as many teachers couldn't navigate the roads, so they canceled several classes.

She used the time to catch up on homework and ask around as to the whereabouts of Travis. His wrestling team hadn't seen him. She figured she'd call him at his home later to bug him about being a pansy.

Her cell phone vibrated just before lunch, and she found a nook in the hallway to answer it. The call was from Melinda.

"What's up, Melinda?"

"Bernadette, I'm kind of worried about Jason, Craig, and Chad," Melinda said.

"Why? What's the matter?"

"Jason didn't drop the van off at my dad's office. He never showed up."

"The weather is miserable, there's hardly anything moving. And, how come you're not at school?" Bernadette asked.

"I've got a head cold. My father's office is in the university hospital, and it's like five minutes from Jason's dorm room," Melinda said.

"Did you call him?"

"Yeah, his phone goes to voice mail."

"He might be sleeping in. I heard Craig and Chad say they wanted to keep watching Ace on their tracker," Bernadette said.

"I hope you're right. How are you holding up today?"

"On pins and needles. I'm second-guessing whether what we did last night was right. I keep thinking I should have left town when the police asked me, instead of involving you in this," Bernadette said.

"Don't worry, we're a behind you," Melinda said. "You did the right thing. Ace will be history, and so will Susie. I'm proud of you, Bernadette."

"Thanks, Melinda. Let's hope it all turns out like a complex math problem where things add up. I'd better go; I've given this number to Travis, and I'm hoping to hear from him," Bernadette said.

She closed her phone and came out into the hallway and ran into Officer Myers.

"Well, Bernadette, just the person I was looking to for," Myers said.

"I didn't realize I was so popular, what's up?" Bernadette asked.

"How about we go to the dojo for a little sparing practice?" Myers wore her street cloths.

"I've got classes."

"Nope, you've got the next two hours free. The teachers didn't make it through the snow. And it's my day off, so you can be my sparing partner."

"Ah, I'm not sure if—"

"No, you are sure—you want to come to the dojo with me. My Jeep outside, and I'll give you a ride back," Myers said. It was a command, not an offer.

"I'll grab my gi," Bernadette said.

Minutes later she was riding through the snow in the Jeep, with Myers chatting nonstop about the storm, how it wasn't that bad, and she had some cool new moves to show Bernadette.

There was no one at the karate School. Myers used her personal key to open the place up. They dressed in their karate gi and came into the dojo, bowing low in reverence before they entered.

"What cool moves do you want to show me?" Bernadette asked.

"The ones to keep you from getting killed."

"What?" Bernadette asked, stopping in mid-stride and looking at Myers.

"Kruger and Salenko saw a strange Town and Country van parked outside a tavern where Ace hangs out. Then they saw it outside the Devil's Undertakers clubhouse. They ran the plates, and it came up belonging to your friend Melinda's mother. How strange is that?"

Bernadette shrugged. "Yeah... pretty strange."

Myers began a series of low punches that Bernadette blocked. They moved forward and back in sparring mode.

"If I find out you, or anyone you're associated with, is interfering with our investigation into Ace and his gang, I'll have you brought up on charges. You know that, don't you?"

"Yes, I'm sure you would," Bernadette said.

"Good." Myers stopped and bowed to Bernadette after they'd finished sparring. "Now, I think I need to show you some things that will stop someone cold."

Bernadette took a breath and looked at Myers. "Why. You think I'm in over my head by staying put and not running?"

Myers grinned. "Yeah, you got me. Exactly what I think. Since you won't run, I'll show you how to disable a person. You've been learning the practical knowledge of karate defense; I'm going to show you how to survive. Stand in front of me."

Bernadette stood facing Myers. She relaxed her breathing and took her karate stance.

"This is outside the *katas* you have learned," Myers said. "You've practiced the basics, now I'm going to show you the stuff that matters." She raised her hand up, the heel touching the base of Bernadette's nose. "This is the palm heel strike. Drive the heel of the hand upward towards the base of the nose. This will stun. Follow it with a strike to both ears with cupped hands." She demonstrated it on Bernadette.

Bernadette felt the air disappear from her ears as Myers placed her hands on both ears. "Wow—effective."

"This is even better." She held onto both of Bernadette's ears. "In this move, you grab both your opponent's ears and pull down hard—you drive their nose into your knee."

"Brilliant move. What's next?"

"Run like hell," Myers said.

"What do you mean, run?"

"Look, there's three Cardinals, and I don't know how many Susie has in her gang, and if you tangle with Ace, he's a nut case—I think he's high on meth half the time. You need to disable and run."

"Okay, fine... what else do you have?"

Myers smiled. "I like your enthusiasm. Now, here's my favorite." She moved to the right of Bernadette and placed the instep of her foot on top and outside of Bernadette's knee. "It takes just under four kilos of pressure to break a knee. You place you foot here, like this, press down hard, you've crippled your assailant."

"Then run like hell?"

"Excellent, you're getting the point."

"I like these." Bernadette moved to Myer's side and tried the foot strike, getting the feel for it.

"Now, this is my favorite, a *nukite zuki,* or finger thrust," Myers said. "I take my hand—it's flat with my thumb tucked to the side. I thrust it hard at someone's eyes. You need to hit hard and come out fast."

"Why?"

"In case you loge a finger inside their eye sockets," Myers said.

"Seriously?"

"The eye is soft, so the finger thrust, when done right, can rupture an eye or blind a person. Now you know why we don't teach this in regular training," Myers said.

"This is outstanding. What else have you got?" Bernadette asked.

"I think you've learned enough for now; let's get you back to class. I've got some paperwork to do back at the precinct. "

Bernadette bowed to Myers. "But what moves do you have if your assailant has a gun?"

"There are no karate moves against a gun," Myers said, raising her hands. "Jackie Chan does it in the movies. The chances of disarming a person who has a weapon on you are slim. You've got to move in close to get the arm holding the gun—it's risky."

"So, put up my hands?" Bernadette said.

"Yeah... our prime suspect, Ace, has had weapons violations in the past. You need to stay away from him. Nothing would stop him from having a gun. You got that?" Myers asked.

"Yeah, I got it, put my hands up," Bernadette said.

"I also said stay away from him."

"I got that too," Bernadette said over her shoulder as she walked to the change room.

She toweled herself off and changed out of her gi, ensuring to fold the garments with reverence into her gym bag. Her sports bra was sopping wet. There was no way she could go out in the cold wearing it. She dug farther into her backpack and found the black lace bra she'd thought she'd lost.

"Just where were you last night?" Bernadette asked the bra. This would have been much more comfortable in her meeting with Ace last night.

"What was that?" Myers asked.

"Ah, nothing, just found some stuff I'd thought I'd lost."

They made their way back to Bernadette's school. Myers held on to Bernadette's arm before she got out of the Jeep. "Here's my card again, in case you lost it. And be careful out there. You seemed to have pissed off many people. I'd like to see you do something special. You're growing on me."

"Thanks." Bernadette smiled, stepped from the Jeep, and made her way into school. Myers was good people; she wished she'd meet her a few months back—she might not have kicked Tommy in the balls.

She was just about to enter French class an hour later when her phone vibrated. The number was unfamiliar. She ducked out into the hall and flipped her phone open.

"Hello..." Bernadette said.

"Bernadette... it's... Travis."

Bernadette relaxed. "Travis, how are you? You must be really sick —because a big strapping guy like you wouldn't let a snow storm stop him."

"You're right, Bernadette—he is a big strapping guy. And he's tied up right now," a voice said.

Bernadette froze. The voice on the phone was Ace.

"What're you doing with Travis?"

A long chuckle came over the phone. "You told quite a tale last night, little girl. How you had the whole wrestling team in your distribution... I just thought I'd do some checking for myself."

The phone went quiet. Bernadette forgot to breathe. "Travis!"

"You don't need to shout. He can hear you just fine. You know, these jocks are kinda dumb, you put a gun to their head, and they'll get into anyone's car," Ace said with a cascade of chuckles.

"What do you want, Ace?"

"That's more like it. Not like the bitch girl from last night now, are we? This is in my house now. Here's what you're going to do. You're going to bring me that flashy five large you showed me last night to a place called Mr. Fixit's Tires on 178th street. I'll give you one hour to get here, otherwise Travis disappears, you got that?"

"I don't have enough time," Bernadette pleaded on the phone.

"Yeah, you have the time. And if you bring any police, Susie here will slit his throat. You got that?" Ace said. "Here, Susie, talk to your friend."

"Hey, girlfriend," Susie said. "Your boy's cute. Maybe I'll give him a little job while I'm waiting—you know—like a blowjob." She chortled into the phone. "And—you know I owe you for last night."

"I'm going to rip your heart out if you touch him, Susie," Bernadette whispered into the phone.

A chorus of laughter came over the phone. Bernadette switched it off and headed for her locker. What was she going to do? If she called Myers, they'd kill Travis. She needed a plan.

It sounded like more than Ace and Susie in the place. She ran back to her locker, threw her books in, and took out her parka. Ace wanted five thousand dollars. She didn't have it. Jason had taken the fake money back. She grabbed some foolscap paper, tore it into thirds, and found a brown envelope. "What does five large look like?" she asked herself. It would be useless, even if she had the fake money, but she could use it as a distraction to get in the door.

She stuffed the envelope in her backpack, threw on her parka, and ran for the exit door. The address Ace gave was over two kilometers away. In this snow, getting there on foot was out of the question. She needed a taxi. The main road with taxis was two blocks over. She did a slow jog towards the door. Her lungs pulled in freezing cold air, her feet descending deep in uneven snow. She hoped she'd be in time.

The main road was almost devoid of traffic as the heavy snow kept falling. Cars and trucks in a single lane were trying to navigate the road.

Bernadette saw a lone taxi on a side road, beside a convenience store. Its engine was running. A figure was inside the steamy windows. She ran the half block towards it, pounding on the driver's window.

"I need a taxi—please—you have to help me!" Bernadette yelled at the window.

The frozen window rolled down slowly. A steam cloud escaped from inside the cab, revealing a dark-skinned man wearing a fur cap and heavy down parka.

"*Is* costing you extra today. The roads—they are crazy," the man said with a thick Spanish accent.

"I need to go twenty blocks from here; see, I have cash," Bernadette said, thrusting a mitt full of twenties at the driver.

The driver shook his head. He put his coffee down on the console and muttered something incomprehensible in Spanish. "Okay, crazy young lady, get in," he said.

Bernadette piled into the back seat. "I need to get to Mr. Fixit's Tires on 178th street," she said out of breath.

"You don't want to pick up your car in weather like this," the cab driver said. He was short and stocky with a large head and wavy black hair. His taxi nameplate stated he was Juan Hernández.

"No, I've got to meet someone, it's really important I get there."

"Okay, you want to be out in this weather, okay by me. You know, for me, I should have stayed home today, but if I do, my wife makes me crazy. So I go out and pick up crazy people like you who want to be in the storm."

Bernadette sat in the back seat and let her mind go over her situation. She'd approach the building—then what? There'd be three, maybe four of them in there. She was going to her own death. She needed to change the odds.

"Is there a hardware store nearby?" she asked.

The cab driver nodded. "Sure, is Canadian Tire, not far away. You want I drop you there instead?"

"No, I want you to take me there and wait for me outside. I need to get something."

"Okay, I don't mind. I sit in my nice warm car and wait for you. Is okay by me. But you have to give me some money. I make sure you come back."

Bernadette pulled out some cash. She had a wad of twenty dollars bills from her recent poker winnings. She slipped two twenties over the seat. "Here's some insurance I come back."

The driver nodded. "Okay by me, I mean no offense."

"None taken."

They stopped outside the large store. Bernadette ran in. She asked someone for directions to camping supplies. It took her a few minutes, but she found exactly what she wanted: a woodsman hatchet, nicely sharpened, and a Buck knife with a four-inch blade and weighted handle.

She would have loved the chance to practice with these, but there was no time. She paid for the items and ran back to the cab.

The cab was sweltering inside. The Spanish cab driver sat huddled in his coat and hat. A small bead of sweat came down from his eyebrow. He brushed it. "We go Mr. Fixit now?"

"Yes," Bernadette said. "We go to Mr. Fixit."

The driver looked in his rearview mirror at Bernadette. "You buy some gifts for your friends."

"Yes, I did, they're a surprise."

28

The cab pulled into traffic. One lane was passable. Snow plows had been by, but the snow was blowing and piling up faster than they could clear it.

Cars followed one another at a safe distance, crawling along the main street with the wind blowing the snow and obliterating vision. Hernandez was an excellent driver; he kept his distance from other cars and maintained his speed.

He drove with caution, but slow, agonizingly slow. Bernadette sweated in the back, from the heat and the tension—would she make it in time? She looked at her cell phone to check the time. Forty-five minutes had gone by since she'd talked to Ace.

Something caught her eye. Her cell-phone power light blinked red. It had no power. How had she let this happen? In her agitated state last night, she'd forgotten to charge it. She'd intended to call Officer Myers just before meeting Ace, so they'd find her while she stalled him.

"We are here," Hernández said.

Bernadette looked up. The cab had arrived outside the Mr. Fixit shop. She hadn't noticed the cab turn off the main road. What was she going to do?

"Do you have a cell phone?" Bernadette asked.

The cabbie shook his head. "No, is too expensive for the calls. If I have one, my wife would call me all day and ask me why I'm not making more money."

Bernadette took officer Myer's card from her pocket. "I need you to do something, Mr. Hernández. I need you to call this number on your cab radio, ask for this officer, and tell her Bernadette needs her." She took out a fifty-dollar bill and handed it to him with the card. "You got that?"

Hernández looked at the police officer's card and the fifty. "You in trouble, little one?"

Bernadette grimaced. "I could be—just trying to be safe. Please let this officer know where you dropped me off."

"*Ai Dios mio*, my little child. I cannot let you go in there on your own."

Bernadette shook her head. "I'm sorry if I'm getting you upset, but it's better I go in alone."

She threw some more cash into the front seat, grabbed her backpack, and got out of the cab. The icy wind grabbed at her the moment she stood outside. The Cadillac with the plates she'd seen outside the school sat parked in the front covered in snow. A faint light shone from inside the building.

The place looked like a repair shop that gone out of business.

A faded oil and lube sign hung over the door. A few empty tire racks bracketed the entrance. Bernadette walked carefully towards the front door and pushed on it. The door opened with a bone-chilling screech. "Shit," Bernadette said softly. Nothing like a major announcement.

She walked into a deserted reception area. A layer of dirt covered scattered papers and overturned chairs. Grease and oil permeated the air. A door with **EMPLOYEES ONLY** had a faint light coming from it.

This was it, she had to go in. She pulled off her backpack to take out the knife and axe. Removing the axe sheath, she stuffed the handle into the waistband of her jeans under her parka. She left the knife in its sheath, removing the strap from the handle. It rested on her hip. Her heart was pounding as she placed her hands on the door.

She pushed the door open. Hands grabbed her, throwing her to the ground. Lights came on. Bernadette shielded her eyes.

David and Leo from Susie's gang stood over her. Their smiles said it all.

29

"Hello, Bernadette," Ace said. "Pull her up boys, check her, make sure she doesn't have any weapons."

The boys pulled Bernadette to her feet. It took them seconds to find her axe and knife and paper bag.

Ace was sitting at a desk in the middle of the shop. They'd scavenged a desk and a leather chair. He looked like he owned the place and was about to do an interview.

Leo took the axe, knife, and dropped them before Ace. He walked back to Bernadette, resuming his grip. "Payback's a bitch," he said with a grin.

"Well," Ace said, looking at the knife and axe. His thumb ran over the axe blade. "Mighty unfriendly to come with weapons to our meeting."

Bernadette eyed Ace and surveyed the room. In the outer edges of the light, she made out the figure of Travis. They had him tied to a chair. Susie sat beside him with a knife balanced on her knee.

"Oh, and look-here," Ace said, dumping the paper onto the desk. "Looks like she came with paper money. Seems you're a liar, little girl."

Susie let out a loud laugh in the corner. It sent a chill up Bernadette's spine.

"Yeah, you're a liar, and you like to meddle in things, don't you, girl," Ace said. He lifted a small tape recorder and punched play. Hoffer's voice came on, *"Okay, kid, leave it to me. I'll make sure Ace is no longer a problem to your school."*

Bernadette's heart did a flip and seemed to have lodged in her throat. She fought hard to breathe.

Ace turned to Susie. "Seems our little friend here figured she'd get me on tape offering to sell to her—what's your take on this, Susie? Strange shit or what?"

"Strange shit, Ace," Susie said.

"And then she figured she run this tape to Carl Hoffer and get him all riled up, have me taken out. You figure you're a pretty clever girl, don't you?" Ace said. He rose from his chair. His hair was hanging down from his head in greasy streaks. His arms were shaking.

Bernadette shrugged. There was no need to answer. She fought hard to concentrate on breathing. Moments remained before her death.

"Well, you figured wrong," Ace said, slamming his palms on the desk. "We spread the word that Hoffer didn't want to sell to schools so people would assume we weren't getting along. Fact is, we're best buddies. You didn't know that, did you?"

Bernadette shook her head. "Guess not."

"Ha, I take care of all the schools in the city. You didn't know that either—did you?"

Bernadette wondered how long this was going to go on. She let herself take in the surroundings, looking for a way out.

"When you came to me, I realized you were lying your little ass off, girl, but I let you do it. You want to know why?"

Bernadette sighed. "Not really, but I you're going to tell me."

"Because we needed a diversion. Tomorrow night we have the biggest crystal meth shipment coming from the coast by truck this town has ever seen. With you and your buddies dead, the cops will be off our back."

The word buddies made Bernadette's skin crawl. "What buddies?"

Ace laughed and slammed the desk hard. "Hit the lights."

The lights came on in the next machine bay. Bernadette gasped as the Town and Country van gleamed in the lights. Three figures sat inside. She made out the profiles of Jason, Chad, and Craig.

"Are they dead?" Bernadette asked in a voice that almost didn't make it past her throat.

"Hell, no, they's just tied up and gagged," Ace said. He walked over and banged on the window. "You okay in there, guys? You just hang tight. They're just the silliest little buggers; they were tailing me last night. Dumb bastards."

Bernadette saw the whites of Chad's eyes in the van. He was shaking his head as if he couldn't believe what they'd gotten into.

"The party's going to start real soon," Ace said, turning with a smile at Bernadette.

"Yep, we gonna have some kind of party, Ace," Susie said.

Bernadette looked at Susie. She had a syringe in her hand.

Ace caught her look. "Recognize this? Pure crystal meth; there's a lethal dose in there. The cops are going to find your bodies shot up with meth like you've been in a hell of a party. Well—some of your bodies," Ace said as a grin spread over his face.

He walked back to his desk. "We plan to shoot you up with meth and put you in the van and torch it. Leave it down by the river—gangland style. The cops will scratch their heads for days, trying to figure out how some high school and university students got that way."

"You'll never get away with this," Bernadette said. "There were to many witnesses in the tavern last night. They'll link my murder to you."

"No, I have this tape you made. I've taken my name out and have you asking for drugs and flashing fake money around. I'll tell the police that sure, I met you. You were looking to make a buy, and that's the last I saw you. They'll find this tape recorder outside the van, with your body, Bernadette," Ace said.

He held up another tape recorder. "This one, this is Carl Hoffer's.

He asked me to make a recording of you pleading for your life. He's a sick bastard. Behind that little guy is one psycho son of a bitch," Ace said.

An involuntary shudder passed through Bernadette's body. Leo and David tightened their grip.

"I told Hoffer I'd investigated your assets before I killed you. You came on pretty strong last night in the tavern. Maybe now is a good time to take you up on your offer," Ace said.

"I never made you any offer." Bernadette said.

"Oh, you said you'd rock my world. Strip her, boys."

Leo grabbed Bernadette's parka and pulled it off. David tore her shirt off. Leo reached around to unhook her bra. Bernadette threw an elbow into his face. He fell back. She lunged forward, placing her boot above his knee. She pressed down hard—he screamed in pain, fell to the ground.

David grabbed her left arm. She wheeled—her fingers flew into his eyes. He dropped, blinded, to the floor.

"Damn. That's good shit, Bernadette," Ace said.

Ace stood at the desk with a gun in his hand.

"Now, what kind of moves have you got for a bullet?"

Bernadette froze. She'd never had a gun pointed at her. Dive for the floor or move left or right were her options. The light switch was behind her. She'd have to get to it before a bullet found her back.

The shop door creaked open. Hernández stepped inside.

"Who the hell are you?" Ace asked.

"I'm this lady's cab driver. My meter is running, and she owes me money... sorry if I intrude. I'll leave now..." He backed up. Bernadette noticed a gun in his hand.

"Bullshit. Stay where you are," Ace yelled. He lifted his gun. Hernandez lifted his. Shots rang out. Hernández fell to the floor.

Bernadette hit the main light switch. The place went dark. She crawled along the floor to Hernández.

"Are you okay?" Bernadette asked in a whisper.

"No, I am shot in the belly. Is no too bad. Here, take my knife, my gun is out of bullets."

Bernadette took the knife. "Did you call the police?"

"Yes, but they say it takes time—the roads are bad. I came to help."

"Lie still," Bernadette said. She felt the wet blood oozing from his bullet wound. She had to deal with Ace.

"I'll be okay." He whispered, "You get that sonofabitch—he looks like an evil man."

"He is bad. I intend to kill him," Bernadette whispered back. She took the knife and crawled along the floor. The light from the outer door showed a path to the desk where Ace had been sitting. Her axe was there. She moved towards it.

A hand grabbed her. She held her breath. She lashed out with the knife. It found a soft body. A loud *ah* told her she'd hit something vital. The hand let go.

She reached the desk, grabbed her axe and knife. The lights came on.

Ace stood at the light switch, his gun aimed at Bernadette. "Here we are again. Looks like your cab driver got a bullet in him—I need to do the same to you."

Bernadette eyed Ace. How far away was he? Six metres read in her mind. Four spins of her axe. Would he shoot her before she threw it?

"Damn it, little girl, I was going to treat you to some quality time before I killed you. Show you what a real man is. But you've put a knife in one my guys and broke Leo's leg—now, we'll just advance to the killing part now."

Bernadette felt the axe handle's weight. She tested it once behind her back. There was no choice.

One stride forward, and the axe flew overhand. Ace brought up his gun to fire. His shot went wide. The axe didn't miss. The blade sunk deep into Ace's chest, splitting his heart in two. He fell backwards.

Bernadette ran to Ace, stood over his body with her knife. She was ready to cut his throat if he reached for his gun. There were no signs of life. She kicked the gun away.

She turned and walked over to Susie. "Drop the knife, Susie."

Susie had her knife at Travis's throat, "I'll slit his throat if you try to take my knife."

Bernadette stopped one metre away from Susie. "I don't need to take your knife. "You see what I did to Ace with my axe. I'm better with a knife—I can plant this in your forehead from this distance. You drop the knife and back away from Travis, or you'll be in a matching body bag with Ace."

Susie stared at Ace on the floor. She dropped the knife and sobbed.

Bernadette approached Travis, jumped on his lap, and showered him with kisses.

"You want to tell me what this is all about?" Travis asked. His tone was harsh—he was in shock.

"I'm so sorry, I didn't mean to involve you in this. I was trying to get Ace in trouble with his gang and it backfired." She jumped up from his lap and cut his ropes off. "I made up a story your wrestling team were helping me move drugs... sorry, it all went wrong."

Sirens sounded, first distant, then closer. Car doors slammed outside, multiple footsteps sounded, until police burst into the room.

Detective Kruger and Officer Myers, gun raised, surveyed the room, transfixed by the scene. Bernadette was covered in blood, wearing jeans and a black lace bra. A young man sat in a chair with Susie bawling nearby.

Three bodies lay on the floor. Ace had an axe protruding from his chest. From blood pooling around him, he looked like a candidate for dead at scene.

Bernadette looked at Myers. "they shot the man by the door. He's the cab driver that brought me. The guy on the floor has a stab wound in the stomach. There are three men in the van. They're okay, just tied up."

Myers motioned for an officer to bring in the EMS team and walked over to Bernadette. "I'm sure you can explain all this."

Bernadette pushed the hair from her eyes, looked at Myers, and sighed.

30

THE NEXT FORTY-EIGHT hours felt like they'd never end. Detectives and Crown Prosecutors interviewed her for hours on end. The questions seemed endless.

"When did you enter the building?" Kruger asked.

"Why did you bring the axe and the knife?" A thin-faced Crown Prosecutor constantly sniffed as Bernadette gave her answers. His name was Boggle, and he reminded Bernadette of a beagle.

"Why didn't you call police right away?" a large-faced lady Crown Prosecutor asked. She took down meticulous notes and kept brushing away a mountain of hair as she did.

After two days, Officer Myers walked into the room. "You're free to go, Bernadette."

"I'm not going to prison for killing Ace?" she asked in disbelief.

"Nope, not for killing Ace, or for stabbing David Feschuck, or breaking Leo Jone's leg. We have cleared you on all charges. Travis and the cab driver's testimony helped, but the tape Ace made while he was intending to kill you was the deciding factor," Myers said. "Oh, and having the police make the biggest drug bust in our city's history, and the arrest of Carl Hoffer and his entire gang—what can I say, you live a charmed life, girl."

Bernadette got up from the chair. Time seemed to have stood still while she was being questioned at police headquarters. She was weary, had slept little, and had eaten sandwiches from the police vending machine.

"Your aunt, cousins, and friends are outside waiting for you. You think you can stay out of trouble until we get you relocated?"

"Relocated, what for?" Bernadette asked, standing by the table in the interview room.

"Don't forget, your life is still in danger from the Cardinal boys. You don't think since you've missed such a close call, you'll be this lucky again, do you?"

Bernadette almost sat down again. She shook her head and stood upright. "Not going to happen. I faced down Ace, I will not back down from Tommy and his idiot cousins."

"You can't kill them with an axe, Bernadette. We let this slide on a one-off basis. You do it again, you got a pattern..."

"No, nothing like that. But I'll need your help—I promise it will be entirely legal," Bernadette said.

* * *

The lights were dim as Tommy Cardinal pushed open the door of the Mr. Fixit's shop. Peter and Stephen were behind him.

"You sure this is where Gus said she'd be?" Peter asked in a halting voice. He hated the dark, wished he'd remembered his flashlight.

"Yeah," Stephen said, "someone phoned Gus at the reservation store and said Bernadette hung out here. She's supposed to be here tonight."

A light came on in the middle of the shop, Bernadette's face illuminated in its glow. "You boys looking for me." She was sitting at a desk with her feet up.

"Ha, there you are, bitch. You tired of running? Decided you want to do all of us before we beat you into the ground?" Tommy asked. He was excited. He had a length of chain in his hands and a large knife.

"I heard a rumor from back home. Someone said you were going to deal with me; you wanted to kill me?"

"You got it, Bernadette," Stephen said. "Tommy here's got some chain and a knife, and I got an axe, and Peter, as dumb as he is, we made him bring a tarp to bundle up your body before we bury you."

"You didn't come to scare me, Stephen? You're fixing to kill me?" Bernadette asked.

Tommy let out a loud laugh. "Hell yeah, Bernadette, my cousin got it right. We mean to rape you, then kill you. This is your last night of hell before we bury you where no one will ever find you."

"Okay, just wanted to get it straight. Lights, please, officers?"

The overhead lights came on. Two police officers with guns raised yelled at Tommy, Peter, and Stephen to raise their hands. Another two officers came through the door behind them. They pushed them to the floor, handcuffed them, and read them their rights.

Peter screamed, "I'm innocent. I didn't want to be in on this—they made me—let me go."

Tommy turned his head where he lay on the floor in handcuffs. "You're a loser, Peter. Be a warrior."

"Warriors don't kill women, Tommy," Bernadette said, staring over the desk at the three boys being taken down. "Weak men kill women, don't you know that? Warriors protect women."

Officer Myers came over to the desk, sat on it, and watched the takedown. "I know you said these kids were stupid, Bernadette, but I didn't think they were *that* stupid."

Bernadette got up from the desk. "What can I say? They should have stayed in school."

31

BERNADETTE WAS CHANGING into her gi at the dojo when Officer Myers walked into the room. They hugged. "I haven't seen you in four months," Bernadette said.

"I've been away on special training. How are you? I hear you're testing today for your orange belt," Myers said.

"Yeah, I'm pretty excited. I hope I get it."

Myer's smiled. "I'm sure you'll pass. How's school?"

"Almost finished. I did my final exam in math today."

Myers pulled her gi out of her gym bag and changed. "So, what does the future hold for Bernadette Callahan? Travel to Europe or Asia? Then to university with some track team?"

Bernadette tied her gi with her yellow belt. "No, track is out for me. My leg injury won't let me train as hard as I want."

"What's your plan?"

"Police studies at MacEwan University."

Myers stopped, dropped her gym bag. "You? Police studies?"

Bernadette laughed. "Yes, me, why not me?"

Myer's smiled. "I figured out police work would be the farthest thing from your mind. Are you planning on joining the city force? I'd be happy to help you."

"No, I've already checked out the RCMP."

"Them, really? You realize they're very military. It's six months' training in Regina. You'll be marching your ass off most of the time. But you'll look good in their brown stetson and red scarlet tunic."

Bernadette chuckled. "My grandmother said she dreamed I was standing in front of a red flag, wearing red. I feel like the RCMP is where I'm meant to be."

"What about Travis? What's he say regarding your choice?"

"Oh, he's long gone..."

"Really, you two broke it off?"

"He didn't enjoy seeing me taking on three guys at Mr. Fixit. I'm not sure he liked me as the warrior princess type."

"It's okay, he's got the white knight syndrome—always wanting to save the damsel. You're just not fragile enough for him."

"I guess not."

"Well, Bernadette, get out there and kick some ass."

"I intend too," Bernadette said, tightening her belt.

"I meant in life," Myers said.

"I got it."

Do you want to know what happens next in Bernadette's story four years later? In the next book, The Hostage Game, Bernadette get's a call for help from Mellissa. Her parents have been kidnapped in Saint Lucia. Will Bernadette put her RCMP career in jeopardy to come to Melissa's aid? Download the Hostage Game now to continue the story!

A FREE SHORT story awaits you! Bernadette Callahan never expected a car chase to lead her into a manhunt in an abandoned mine. Can she find her way out and find the criminal before it's too late? Click here to claim your copy of Treading Darkness today to find out what happens next.

~

NEXT IN SERIES

When Bernadette's friends are taken hostage in Saint Lucia, she rushes to help. But the only way she can find the hostages is if she puts her life in danger. Will she do it?

Events will unfold that will make her doubt herself and her instincts. The kidnappers are always one step ahead. They're playing a deadly game with the hostages as their pawns.

Let your senses be taken back to the tropical island of Saint Lucia in year 2000 as a young Bernadette Callahan is given her first challenge before entering the RCMP. She's not only putting her life on the line, but her career as well. If she uses deadly force, she sacrifices her career in law enforcement.

Download this book now to start reading this fast action journey!

DEAR READER
SOME NOTES ON THE BOOK

I hope you enjoyed this book. I wrote this book to give readers a sense of where Bernadette Callahan came from and the struggles she went through to get to where she is now in the rest of the series.

I used the backdrop of the city of Edmonton, in northern Canada where I grew up. I included an actual school I attended for one year, where 'ass kicking,' really was on the menu. To survive, I had to talk fast and make friends with some really tough kids. As you saw in the book, Bernadette did it differently, then, she always does.

If you enjoyed the book, perhaps you'd like others know about it as well. Please leave a review here if you wish.

ACKNOWLEDGMENTS

I wish to thank my good friend, Rhonda Alderson who assisted me with the techniques of Goju ryu Karate, of which she attained a second degree black belt. I also thank her profusely for not injuring me in showing the moves.

And, I'd never be very far in my writing without the guidance of Joe Nahman, an excellent criminal lawyer with great insights and a sense of humor to match.

To my beta readers, Stan Shaw, Dr. Murray Allen, Rhonda Alderson and my wife, Tessa, I'm always in your debt for the feedback.

ABOUT THE AUTHOR

Lyle Nicholson is the author of nine novels, two novellas and a short story, as well a contributor of freelance articles to several newspapers and magazines in Canada.

In his former life, he was a bad actor in a Johnny Cash movie, Gospel Road, a disobedient monk in a monastery and a failure in working for others.

He would start his own successful sales agency and retire to write full time in 2011. The many characters and stories that have resided inside his head for years are glad he did.

He lives in Kelowna, British Columbia, Canada with his lovely wife of many years where he indulges in his passion for writing, cooking and fine wines.

ALSO BY LYLE NICHOLSON

For a complete and up-to-date list of Lyle Nicholson's releases, please visit his website at

www.lylenicholson.com